Oldtown Fireside Stories

Harriet Beecher Stowe

Complete & Unabridged

Tutis Digital Publishing Private Limited

First published in 1872 as *Oldtown Fireside Stories.*

The Ghost in the Mill

"Come, Sam, tell us a story," said I, as Harry and I crept to his knees, in the glow of the bright evening firelight; while Aunt Lois was busily rattling the tea-things, and grandmamma, at the other end of the fireplace, was quietly setting the heel of a blue-mixed yarn stocking.

In those days we had no magazines and daily papers, each reeling off a serial story. Once a week, "The Columbian Sentinel" came from Boston with its slender stock of news and editorial; but all the multiform devices – pictorial, narrative, and poetical – which keep the mind of the present generation ablaze with excitement, had not then even an existence. There was no theatre, no opera; there were in Oldtown no parties or balls, except, perhaps, the annual election, or Thanksgiving festival; and when winter came, and the sun went down at half-past four o'clock, and left the long, dark hours of evening to be provided for, the necessity of amusement became urgent. Hence, in those days, chimney-corner story-telling became an art and an accomplishment. Society then was full of traditions and narratives which had all the uncertain glow and shifting mystery of the firelit hearth upon them. They were told to sympathetic audiences, by the rising and falling light of the solemn embers, with the hearth-crickets filling up every pause. Then the aged told their stories to the young, – tales of early life; tales of war and adventure, of forest-days, of Indian captivities and escapes, of bears and wild-cats and panthers, of rattlesnakes, of witches and wizards, and strange and wonderful dreams and appearances and providences.

In those days of early Massachusetts, faith and credence were in the very air. Two-thirds of New England was then dark, unbroken forests, through whose tangled paths the mysterious winter wind groaned and shrieked and howled with weird noises and unaccountable clamors. Along the iron-bound shore, the stormful Atlantic raved and thundered, and dashed its moaning waters, as if to deaden and deafen any voice that might tell of the settled life of the old civilized world, and shut us forever into the wilderness. A good story-teller, in those days, was always sure of a warm seat at the hearthstone, and the delighted homage of children; and in all Oldtown there was no better story-teller than Sam Lawson.

"Do, do, tell us a story," said Harry, pressing upon him, and opening very wide blue eyes, in which undoubting faith shone as in a mirror; "and let it be something strange, and different from common."

"Wal, I know lots o' strange things," said Sam, looking mysteriously into the fire. "Why, I know things, that ef I should tell, – why, people might day they wa'n't so; but then they *is* so for all that."

"Oh, *do*, do, tell us!"

"Why, I should scare ye to death, mebbe," said Sam doubtingly.

"Oh, pooh! no, you wouldn't," we both burst out at once.

But Sam was possessed by a reticent

spirit, and loved dearly to be wooed and importuned; and so he only took up the great kitchen-tongs, and smote on the hickory forestick, when it flew apart in the middle, and scattered a shower of clear bright coals all over the hearth.

"Mercy on us, Sam Lawson!" said Aunt Lois in an indignant voice, spinning round from her dishwashing.

"Don't you worry a grain, Miss Lois," said Sam composedly. "I see that are stick was e'en a'most in two, and I thought I'd jest settle it. I'll sweep up the coals now," he added, vigorously applying a turkey-wing to the purpose, as he knelt on the hearth, his spare, lean figure glowing in the blaze of the firelight, and getting quite flushed with exertion.

"There, now!" he said, when he had brushed over and under and between the fire-irons, and pursued the retreating ashes so far into the red, fiery citadel, that his finger-ends were burning and tingling, "that are's done now as well as Hepsy herself could 'a' done it. I allers sweeps up the haarth: I think it's part o'

4

the man's bisness when he makes the fire. But Hepsy's so used to seein' me a-doin' on't, that she don't see no kind o' merit in't. It's just as Parson Lothrop said in his sermon, – folks allers overlook their common marcies" –

"But come, Sam, that story," said Harry and I coaxingly, pressing upon him, and pulling him down into his seat in the corner.

"Lordy massy, these 'ere young uns!" said Sam. "There's never no contentin' on 'em: ye tell 'em one story, and they jest swallows it as a dog does a gob o' meat; and they're all ready for another. What do ye want to hear now?"

Now, the fact was, that Sam's stories had been told us so often, that they were all arranged and ticketed in our minds. We knew every word in them, and could set him right if he varied a hair from the usual track; and still the interest in them was unabated. Still we shivered, and clung to his knee, at the mysterious parts, and felt gentle, cold chills run down our spines at appropriate places. We were always in the most receptive and sympathetic condition. To-night, in particular, was one of those thundering stormy ones, when the winds appeared to be holding a perfect mad carnival over my grandfather's house. They yelled and squealed round the corners; they collected in troops, and came tumbling and roaring down chimney; they shook and tattled the buttery-door and the sinkroom-door and the cellar-door and the chamber-door, with a constant undertone of squeak and clatter, as if at every door were a cold, discontented spirit, tired of the chill outside, and longing for the warmth and comfort within.

"Wal, boys," said Sam confidentially, "what'll ye have?"

"Tell us 'Come down, come down!'" we both shouted with one voice. This was, in our mind, an "A No. 1" among Sam's stories.

"Ye mus'n't be frightened now," said Sam paternally.

"Oh, no! we ar'n't frightened ever," said we both in one breath.

"Not when ye go down the cellar arler cider?" said Sam with severe scrutiny. "Ef ye should be down cellar, and the candle should go out, now?"

"I ain't," said I: "I ain't afraid of any thing. I never knew what it was to be afraid in my life."

"Wal, then," said Sam, "I'll tell ye. This 'ere's what Cap'n Eb Sawin told me when I was a boy about your bigness, I reckon.

"Cap'n Eb Sawin was a most respectable man. Your gran'ther knew him very well; and he was a deacon in the church in Dedham afore he died. He was at Lexington when the fust gun was fired agin the British. He was a dreffle smart man, Cap'n Eb was, and driv team a good many years atween here and Boston. He married Lois Peabody, that was cousin to your gran'ther then. Lois was a rael sensible woman; and I've heard her tell the story as he told her, and it was jest as he told it to me, – jest exactly; and I shall never forget it if I live to be nine hundred years old, like Mathuselah.

"Ye see, along back in them times, there used to be a fellow come round these

7

'ere parts, spring and fall, a-peddlin' goods, with his pack on his back; and his name was Jehiel Lommedieu. Nobody rightly knew where he come from. He wasn't much of a talker; but the women rather liked him, and kind o' liked to have him round. Women will like some fellows, when men can't see no sort o' reason why they should; and they liked this 'ere Lommedieu, though he was kind o' mournful and thin and shad-bellied, and hadn't nothin' to say for himself. But it got to be so, that the women would count and calculate so many weeks afore 'twas time for Lommedieu to be along; and they'd make up ginger-snaps and preserves and pies, and make him stay to tea at the houses, and feed him up on the best there was: and the story went round, that he was a-courtin' Phebe Ann Parker, or Phebe Ann was a-courtin' him, – folks didn't rightly know which. Wal, all of a sudden, Lommedieu stopped comin' round; and nobody knew why, – only jest he didn't come. It turned out that Phebe Ann Parker had got a letter from him, sayin' he'd be along afore Thanksgiving; but he didn't come, neither afore nor at

Thanksgiving time, nor arter, nor next spring: and finally the women they gin up lookin' for him. Some said he was dead; some said he was gone to Canada; and some said he hed gone over to the Old Country.

"Wal, as to Phebe Ann, she acted like a gal o' sense, and married 'Bijah Moss, and thought no more 'bout it. She took the right view on't, and said she was sartin that all things was ordered out for the best; and it was jest as well folks couldn't always have their own way. And so, in time, Lommedieu was gone out o' folks's minds, much as a last year's apple-blossom.

"It's relly affectin' to think how little these 'ere folks is missed that's so much sot by. There ain't nobody, ef they's ever so important, but what the world gets to goin' on without 'em, pretty much as it did with 'em, though there's some little flurry at fust. Wal, the last thing that was in anybody's mind was, that they ever should hear from Lommedieu agin. But there ain't nothin' but what has its time o' turnin' up; and it seems his turn was to come.

"Wal, ye see, 'twas the 19th o' March, when Cap'n Eb Sawin started with a team for Boston. That day, there come on about the biggest snow-storm that there'd been in them parts sence the oldest man could remember. 'Twas this 'ere fine, siftin' snow, that drives in your face like needles, with a wind to cut your nose off: it made teamin' pretty tedious work. Cap'n Eb was about the toughest man in them parts. He'd spent days in the woods a-loggin', and he'd been up to the deestrict o' Maine a-lumberin', and was about up to any sort o' thing a man gen'ally could be up to; but these 'ere March winds sometimes does set on a fellow so, that neither natur' nor grace can stan' 'em. The cap'n used to say he could stan' any wind that blew one way 't time for five minutes; but come to winds that blew all four p'ints at the same minit, – why, they flustered him.

"Wal, that was the sort o' weather it was all day: and by sundown Cap'n Eb he got clean bewildered, so that he lost his road; and, when night came on, he didn't know nothin' where he was. Ye see the country was all under drift, and the air so thick with snow, that he couldn't see a foot afore him; and the fact was, he got off the Boston road without knowin' it, and came out at a pair o' bars nigh upon Sherburn, where old Cack Sparrock's mill is.

"Your gran'ther used to know old Cack, boys. He was a drefful drinkin' old crittur, that lived there all alone in the woods by himself a-tendin' saw and grist mill. He wasn't allers jest what he was then. Time was that Cack was a pretty consid'ably likely young man, and his wife was a very respectable woman, – Deacon Amos Petengall's dater from Sherburn.

"But ye see, the year arter his wife died, Cack he gin up goin' to meetin' Sundays, and, all the tithing-men and selectmen could do, they couldn't get him out to meetin'; and, when a man neglects means o' grace and sanctuary privileges, there ain't no sayin' *what* he'll do next. Why, boys, jist think on't! – an immortal crittur lyin' round loose all day Sunday, and not puttin' on so much as a clean shirt, when all 'spectable folks has on their best close, and is to meetin' worshippin' the Lord! What can you spect to come of it, when he lies idlin' round in his old week-day close, fishing, or some sich, but what the Devil should be arter him at last, as he was arter old Cack?"

Here Sam winked impressively to my grandfather in the opposite corner, to call his attention to the moral which he was interweaving with his narrative.

"Wal, ye see, Cap'n Eb he told me, that when he come to them bars and looked up, and saw the dark a-comin' down, and the storm a-thickenin' up, he felt that things was gettin' pretty consid'able serious. There was a dark piece o' woods on ahead of him inside the bars; and he knew, come to get in there, the light would give out clean. So he jest thought he'd take the hoss out o' the team, and go ahead a little, and see where he was. So he driv his oxen up ag'in the fence, and took out the hoss, and got on him, and pushed along through the woods, not rightly knowin' where he was goin'.

"Wal, afore long he see a light through the trees; and, sure enough, he come out to Cack Sparrock's old mill.

"It was a pretty consid'able gloomy sort of a place, that are old mill was. There was a great fall of water that come rushin' down the rocks, and fell in a deep pool; and it sounded sort o' wild and lonesome: but Cap'n Eb he knocked on the door with his whip-handle, and got in.

"There, to be sure, sot old Cack beside a great blazin' fire, with his rum-jug at his elbow. He was a drefful fellow to drink, Cack was! For all that, there was some good in him, for he was pleasant-spoken and 'bliging; and he made the cap'n welcome.

"'Ye see, Cack,' said Cap'n Eb, 'I 'm off my road, and got snowed up down by your bars,' says he.

"'Want ter know!' says Cack. 'Calculate you'll jest have to camp down here till mornin',' says he.

"Wal, so old Cack he got out his tin lantern, and went with Cap'n Eb back to the bars to help him fetch along his critturs. He told him he could put 'em under the mill-shed. So they got the critturs up to the shed, and got the cart under; and by that time the storm was awful.

"But Cack he made a great roarin' fire, 'cause, ye see, Cack allers had slab-wood a plenty from his mill; and a roarin' fire is jest so much company. It sort o' keeps a fellow's spirits up, a good fire does. So Cack he sot on his old teakettle, and made a swingeing lot o' toddy; and he and Cap'n Eb were havin' a tol'able comfortable time there. Cack was a pretty good hand to tell stories; and Cap'n Eb warn't no way backward in that line, and kep' up his end pretty well: and pretty soon they was a-roarin' and haw-hawin' inside about as loud as the storm outside; when all of a sudden, 'bout midnight, there come a loud rap on the door.

"'Lordy massy! what's that?' says Cack. Folks is rather startled allers to be checked up sudden when they are a-carryin' on and laughin'; and it was such an awful blowy night, it was a little scary to have a rap on the door.

"Wal, they waited a minit, and didn't hear nothin' but the wind a-screechin' round the chimbley; and old Cack was jest goin' on with his story, when the rap come ag'in, harder'n ever, as if it'd shook the door open.

"'Wal,' says old Cack,' if 'tis the Devil, we'd jest as good's open, and have it out with him to onst,' says he; and so he got up and opened the door, and, sure enough, there was old Ketury there. Expect you've heard your grandma tell about old Ketury. She used to come to meetin's sometimes, and her husband was one o' the prayin' Indians; but Ketury was one of the rael wild sort, and you couldn't no more convert *her* than you could convert a wild-cat or a painter [panther]. Lordy massy! Ketury used to come to meetin', and sit there on them Indian benches; and when the second bell was a-tollin', and when Parson Lothrop and his wife was comin' up the broad aisle, and everybody in the house ris' up and stood, Ketury would sit there, and look at 'em out o' the corner o' her eyes; and folks used to say she rattled them necklaces o' rattlesnakes' tails and wild-cat teeth, and sich like heathen trumpery, and looked for all the world as if the spirit of the old Sarpent himself was in her. I've seen her sit and look at Lady Lothrop out o' the corner o' her eyes; and her old brown baggy neck would kind o' twist and work; and her eyes they looked so, that 'twas enough to scare a body. For all the world, she looked jest as if she was a-workin' up to spring at her. Lady Lothrop was jest as kind to Ketury as she always was to every poor crittur. She'd bow and smile as gracious to her when meetin' was over, and she come down the aisle, passin' oot o, meetin'; but Ketury never took no notice. Ye see, Ketury's father was one o' them great powwows down to Martha's Vineyard; and people used to say she was set apart, when she was a child, to the sarvice o' the Devil: any way, she never could be made nothin' of in a Christian way. She come down to Parson Lothrop's study once or twice to be catechised; but he couldn't get a word out o' her, and she kind o' seemed to sit scornful while he was a-talkin'. Folks said, if it was in old times, Ketury wouldn't have been allowed to go on so; but Parson Lothrop's so sort o' mild, he let her take pretty much her own way. Everybody thought that Ketury was a witch: at least, she knew consid'able more'n she ought to know, and so they was kind o' 'fraid on her. Cap'n Eb says he never see a fellow seem scareder than Cack did when he see Ketury a-standin' there.

"Why, ye see, boys, she was as withered and wrinkled and brown as an old frosted punkin-vine; and her little snaky eyes sparkled and snapped, and it made yer head kind o' dizzy to look at 'em; and folks used to say that anybody that Ketury got mad at was sure to get the worst of it fust or last. And so, no matter what day or hour Ketury had a mind to rap at anybody's door, folks gen'lly thought it was best to let her in; but then, they never thought her coming was for any good, for she was just like the wind, – she came when the fit was on her, she staid jest so long as it pleased her, and went when she got ready, and not before. Ketury understood English, and could talk it well enough, but always seemed to scorn it, and was allers mo win' and mutterin' to herself in Indian, and winkin' and blinkin' as if she saw more-folks round than you did, so that she

17

wa'n't no way pleasant company; and yet everybody took good care to be polite to her. So old Cack asked her to come in, and didn't make-no question where she come from, or what she come on; but he knew it was twelve good miles from where she lived to his hut, and the snow was drifted above her middle: and Cap'n Eb declared that there wa'n't no track, nor sign o' a track, of anybody's coming through that snow next morning."

"How did she get there, then?" said I.

"Didn't ye never see brown leaves a-ridin' on the wind? Well,' Cap'n Eb he says, 'she came on the wind,' and I'm sure it was strong enough to fetch her. But Cack he got her down into the warm corner, and he poured her out a mug o' hot toddy, and give her: but ye see her bein' there sort o' stopped the conversation; for she sot there a-rockin' back'ards and for'ards, a-sippin her toddy, and a-mutterin', and lookin' up chimbley.

"Cap'n Eb says in all his born days he never hearn such screeches and yells as the wind give over that chimbley; and old Cack got so frightened, you could fairly hear his teeth chatter.

"But Cap'n Eb he was a putty brave man, and he wa'n't goin' to have conversation stopped by no woman, witch or no witch; and so, when he see her mutterin', and lookin' up chimbley, he spoke up, and says he, 'Well, Ketury, what do you see?' says he. 'Come, out with it; don't keep it to yourself.' Ye see Cap'n Eb was a hearty fellow, and then he was a leetle warmed up with the toddy.

"Then he said he see an evil kind o' smile on Ketury's face, and she rattled her necklace o' bones and snakes' tails; and her eyes seemed to snap; and she looked up the chimbley, and called out, 'Come down, come down! let's see who ye be.'

"Then there was a scratchin' and a rumblin' and a groan; and a pair of feet come down the chimbley, and stood right in the middle of the haarth, the toes pi'ntin' out'rds, with shoes and silver buckles a-shin-in' in the firelight. Cap'n Eb says he never come so near bein' scared in his life; and, as to old Cack, he jest wilted right down in his chair.

"Then old Ketury got up, and reached her stick up chimbley, and called out louder, 'Come down, come down! let's see who ye be.' And, sure enough, down came a pair o' legs, and j'ined right on to the feet: good fair legs they was, with ribbed stockings and leather breeches.

"'Wal, we're in for it now,' says Cap'n Eb. 'Go it, Ketury, and let's have the rest on him.'

"Ketury didn't seem to mind him: she stood there as stiff as a stake, and kep' callin' out, 'Come down, come down! let's see who ye be.' And then come down the body of a man with a brown coat and yellow vest, and j'ined right on to the legs; but there wa'n't no arms to it. Then Ketury shook her stick up chimbley, and called, '*Come down, come down!*' And there came down a pair o' arms, and went on each side o' the body; and there stood a man all finished, only there wa'n't no head on him.

"'Wal, Ketury,' says Cap'n Eb, 'this 'ere's

getting serious. I 'spec' you must finish him up, and let's see what he wants of us.'

"Then Ketury called out once more, louder'n ever, 'Come down, come down! let's see who ye be.' And, sure enough, down comes a man's head, and settled on the shoulders straight enough; and Cap'n Eb, the minit he sot eyes on him, knew he was Jehiel Lommedieu.

"Old Cack knew him too; and he fell flat on his face, and prayed the Lord to have mercy on his soul: but Cap'n Eb he was for gettin' to the bottom of matters, and not have his scare for nothin'; so he says to him, 'What do you want, now you hev come?'

"The man he didn't speak; he only sort o' moaned, and p'inted to the chimbley. He seemed to try to speak, but couldn't; for ye see it isn't often that his sort o' folks is permitted to speak: but just then there came a screechin' blast o' wind, and blowed the door open, and blowed the smoke and fire all out into the room, and there seemed to be a whirlwind and darkness and moans and screeches; and, when it all cleared up, Ketury and the man was both gone, and only old Cack lay on the ground, rolling and moaning as if he'd die.

"Wal, Cap'n Eb he picked him up, and built up the fire, and sort o' comforted him up, 'cause the crit-tur was in distress o' mind that was drefful. The awful Providence, ye see, had awakened him, and his sin had been set home to his soul; and he was under such conviction, that it all had to come out, – how old Cack's father had murdered poor Lommedieu for his money, and Cack had been privy to it, and helped his father build the body up in that very chimbley; and he said that he hadn't had neither peace nor rest since then, and that was what had driv' him away from ordinances; for ye know sinnin' will always make a man leave prayin'. Wal, Cack didn't live but a day or two. Cap'n Eb he got the minister o' Sherburn and one o' the selectmen down to see him; and they took his deposition. He seemed railly quite penitent; and Parson Carryl he prayed with him, and was faithful in settin' home the providence to his soul: and so, at the eleventh hour, poor old

Cack might have got in; at least it looks a leetle like it. He was distressed to think he couldn't live to be hung. He sort o' seemed to think, that if he was fairly tried, and hung, it would make it all square. He made Parson Carryl promise to have the old mill pulled down, and bury the body; and, after he was dead, they did it.

"Cap'n Eb he was one of a party o' eight that pulled down the chimbley; and there, sure enough, was the skeleton of poor Lommedieu.

"So there you see, boys, there can't be no iniquity so hid but what it'll come out. The Wild Indians of the forest, and the stormy winds and tempests, j'ined together to bring out this 'ere."

"For my part," said Aunt Lois sharply, "I never believed that story."

"Why, Lois," said my grandmother, "Cap'n Eb Sawin was a regular church-member, and a most respectable man."

"Law, mother! I don't doubt he thought so. I suppose he and Cack got drinking toddy together, till he got asleep, and dreamed it. I wouldn't believe such a thing if it did happen right before my face and eyes. I should only think I was crazy, that's all."

"Come, Lois, if I was you, I wouldn't talk so like a Sadducee," said my grandmother. "What would become of all the accounts in Dr. Cotton Mather's 'Magnilly' if folks were like you?"

"Wal," said Sam Lawson, drooping contemplatively over the coals, and gazing into the fire, "there's a putty consid'able sight o' things in this world that's true; and then ag'in there's a sight o' things that ain't true. Now, my old gran'ther used to say, 'Boys, says he, 'if ye want to lead a pleasant and prosperous life, ye must contrive allers to keep jest the *happy medium* between truth and falsehood.' Now, that are's my doctrine."

Aunt Lois knit severely.

"Boys," said Sam, "don't you want ter go down with me and get a mug o' cider?"

Of course we did, and took down a

basket to bring up some apples to roast.

"Boys," says Sam mysteriously, while he was drawing the cider, "you jest ask your Aunt Lois to tell you what she knows 'bout Ruth Sullivan."

"Why, what is it?"

"Oh! you must ask her. These 'ere folks that's so kind o' toppin' about sperits and sich, come sift 'em down, you gen'lly find they knows one story that kind o' puzzles 'em. Now you mind, and jist ask your Aunt Lois about Ruth Sullivan."

The Sullivan Looking-Glass

"Aunt Lois," said I, "what was that story about Ruth Sullivan?"

Aunt Lois's quick black eyes gave a looked at each other a minute significantly. "Who told you any thing about Ruth Sullivan," she said sharply.

"Nobody. Somebody said *you* knew something about her," said I.

I was holding a skein of yarn for Aunt Lois; and she went on winding in silence, putting the ball through loops and tangled places.

"Little boys shouldn't ask questions," she concluded at last sententiously. "Little boys that ask too many questions get sent to bed."

I knew that of old, and rather wondered at my own hardihood.

Aunt Lois wound on in silence; but, looking in her face, I could see plainly that I had started an exciting topic.

"I should think," pursued my

grandmother in her corner, "that Ruth's case might show you, Lois, that a good many things may happen, – more than you believe."

"Oh, well, mother! Ruth's was a strange case; but I suppose there are ways of accounting for it."

"You believed Ruth, didn't you?"

"Oh, certainly, I believed Ruth! Why shouldn't I? Ruth was one of my best friends, and as true a girl as lives: there wasn't any nonsense about Ruth. She was one of the sort," said Aunt Lois reflectively, "that I'd as soon trust as myself: when she said a thing was so and so, I knew it was so."

"Then, if you think Ruth's story was true," pursued my grandmother, "what's the reason you are always cavilling at things just 'cause you can't understand how they came to be so?"

Aunt Lois set her lips firmly, and wound with grim resolve. She was the very impersonation of that obstinate rationalism that grew up at the New-England fireside, close alongside of the most undoubting faith in the supernatural.

"I don't believe such things," at last she snapped out, "and I don't disbelieve them. I just let 'em alone. What do I know about 'em? Ruth tells me a story; and I believe her. I know what she saw beforehand, came true in a most remarkable way. Well, I'm sure I've no objection. One thing may be true, or another, for all me; but, just because I believe Ruth Sullivan, I'm not going to believe, right and left, all the stories in Cotton Mather, and all that anybody can hawk up to tell. Not I."

This whole conversation made me all the more curious to get at the story thus dimly indicated; and so we beset Sam for information.

"So your Aunt Lois wouldn't tell ye nothin'," said Sam. "Wanter know, neow! sho!"

"No: she said we must go to bed if we asked her."

"That 'are's a way folks has; but, ye see, boys," said Sam, while a droll confidential expression crossed the lack-lustre dolefulness of his visage, "ye see, I put ye up to it, 'cause Miss Lois is so large and commandin' in her ways, and so kind o' up and down in all her doin's, that I like once and a while to sort o' gravel her; and I knowed enough to know that that 'are question would git her in a tight place.

"Ye see, yer Aunt Lois was knowin' to all this 'ere about Ruth, so there wer'n't no gettin' away from it; and it's about as remarkable a providence as any o' them of Mister Cotton Marther's 'Magnilly.' So if you'll come up in the barn-chamber this arternoon, where I've got a lot o' flax to hatchel out, I'll tell ye all about it."

So that afternoon beheld Sam arranged at full length on a pile of top-tow in the barn-chamber, hatchelling by proxy by putting Harry and myself to the service.

"Wal, now, boys, it's kind o' refreshing to see how wal ye take hold," he observed. "Nothin' like bein' industrious while ye'r young: gret sight better now than loafin off, down in them medders.

"'In books and work and useful play
Let my fust years be past:
So shall I give for every day
Some good account at last.'"

"But, Sam, if we work for you, you must tell us that story about Ruth Sullivan."

"Lordy massy! yis, – course I will. I've had the best kind o' chances of knowin' all about that 'are. Wal, you see there was old Gineral Sullivan, he lived in state and grande'r in the old Sullivan house out to Roxberry. I been to Roxberry, and seen that 'are house o' Gineral Sullivan's. There was one time that I was a consid'able spell lookin' round in Roxberry, a kind o' seein' how things wuz there, and whether or no there mightn't be some sort o' providential openin' or suthin'. I used to stay with Aunt Polly Ginger. She was sister to Mehitable Ginger, Gineral Sullivan's housekeeper, and hed the in and out o' the Sullivan house, and kind o' kept the run o' how things went and came in it. Polly she was a kind o' cousin o' my mother's, and allers glad to see me. Fact was, I was putty handy round house; and she used to save up her broken things and sich till I come round in the fall; and then I'd mend 'em up, and put the clock right, and split her up a lot o' kindlings, and board up the cellar-windows, and kind o' make her sort o' comfortable, – she bein' a lone body, and no man round. As I said, it was sort o' convenient to hev me; and so I jest got the run o' things in the Sullivan house pretty much as ef I was one on 'em, Gineral Sullivan he kept a grand house, I tell you. You see, he cum from the old country, and felt sort o' lordly and grand; and they used to hev the gretest kind o' doin's there to the Sullivan house. Ye ought ter a seen that 'are house, – gret big front hall and gret wide stairs; none o' your steep kind that breaks a feller's neck to get up and down, but gret broad stairs with easy risers, so they used to say you could a cantered a pony up that 'are stairway easy as not. Then there was gret wide rooms, and sofys, and curtains, and gret curtained bedsteads that looked sort o' like fortifications, and pictur's that was got in Italy and Rome and all them 'are heathen places. Ye see, the Gineral was a drefful worldly old critter, and was all for the pomps and the vanities. Lordy massy! I wonder what the poor old critter thinks about it all now, when his body's all gone to dust and ashes in the graveyard, and his soul's gone to 'tarnity! Wal, that are ain't none o' my business; only it shows the vanity o' riches in a kind o' strikin' light, and makes me content that I never hed none."

"But, Sam, I hope General Sullivan wasn't a wicked man, *was* he?"

"Wal, I wouldn't say he was railly wickeder than the run; but he was one o' these 'ere high-stepping, big-feeling fellers, that seem to be a hevin' their portion in this life. Drefful proud he was; and he was pretty much sot on this world, and kep' a sort o' court goin' on round him. Wal, I don't jedge him nor nobody: folks that hes the world is apt to get sot on it. Don't none on us do more than middlin' well."

"But, Sam, what about Ruth Sullivan?"

"Ruth? – Oh, yis! – Ruth –

"Wal, ye see, the only crook in the old

Gineral's lot was he didn't hev no children. Mis' Sullivan, she was a beautiful woman, as handsome as a pictur'; but she never had but one child; and he was a son who died when he was a baby, and about broke her heart. And then this 'ere Ruth was her sister's child, that was born about the same time; and, when the boy died, they took Ruth home to sort o' fill his place, and kind o' comfort up Mis' Sullivan. And then Ruth's father and mother died; and they adopted her for their own, and brought her up.

"Wal, she grew up to be amazin' handsome. Why, everybody said that she was jest the light and glory of that 'are old Sullivan place, and worth more'n all the pictur's and the silver and the jewels, and all there was in the house; and she was jest so innercent and sweet, that you never see nothing to beat it. Wal, your Aunt Lois she got acquainted with Ruth one summer when she was up to Old Town a visitin' at Parson Lothrop's. Your Aunt Lois was a gal then, and a pretty good-lookin' one too; and, somehow or other, she took to Ruth, and Ruth took to her. And when Ruth went home, they used to be a writin' backwards and forads; and I guess the fact was, Ruth thought about as much of your Aunt Lois as she did o' anybody. Ye see, your aunt was a kind o' strong up-and-down woman that always knew certain jest what she did know; and Ruth, she was one o' them gals that seems sort o' like a stray lamb or a dove that's sort o' lost their way in the world, and wants some one to show 'em where to go next. For, ye see, the fact was, the old Gineral and Madam, they didn't agree very well. He wa'n't well pleased that she didn't have no children; and she was sort o' jealous o' him 'cause she got hold o' some sort of story about how he was to a married somebody else over there in England: so she got sort o' riled up, jest as wim-men will, the best on 'em; and they was pretty apt to have spats, and one could give t'other as good as they sent; and, by all accounts, they fit putty lively sometimes. And, between the two, Ruth she was sort o' scared, and fluttered like a dove that didn't know jest where to settle. Ye see, there she was in; that 'are great wide house, where they was a feastin' and a prancin' and a dancin', and a goin' on like Ahashuerus and Herodias and all them old Scripture days. There was acomin' and goin,' and there was gret dinners and gret doin's, but no love; and, you know, the Scriptur' says, 'Better is a dinner o' yarbs, where love is, than a stalled ox, and hatred therewith.'

"Wal, I don't orter say *hatred*, arter all. I kind o' reckon, the old Gineral did the best he could: the fact is, when a woman gits a kink in her head agin a man, the best on us don't allers do jest the right thing.

"Any way, Ruth, she was sort o' forlorn, and didn't seem to take no comfort in the goin's on. The Gineral he was mighty fond on her, and proud on her; and there wa'n't nothin' too good for Ruth. He was free-handed, the Gineral wuz. He dressed her up in silks and satins, and she hed a maid to wait on her, and she hed sets o' pearl and dimond; and Madam Sullivan she thought all the world on her, and kind o' worshipped the ground she trod on. And yet Ruth was sort o' lonesome.

"Ye see, Ruth wa'n't calculated for grande'r. Some folks ain't.

"Why, that 'are summer she spent out to Old Town, she was jest as chirk and chipper as a wren, a wearin' her little sun-bunnet, and goin' a huckle-berryin' and a black-berryin' and diggin' sweet-flag, and gettin cowslops and dandelions; and she hed a word for everybody. And everybody liked Ruth, and wished her well. Wal, she was sent for her health; and she got that, and more too: she got a sweetheart.

"Ye see, there was a Cap'n Oliver a visitin' at the minister's that summer, – a nice, handsome young man as ever was. He and Ruth and your Aunt Lois, they was together a good deal; and they was a ramblin' and a ridin' and a sailin': and so Ruth and the Capting went the way o' all the airth, and fell dead in love with each other. Your Aunt Lois she was knowing to it and all about it, 'cause Ruth she was jest one of them that couldn't take a step without somebody to talk to.

"Captain Oliver was of a good family in

England; and so, when he made bold to ask the old Gineral for Ruth, he didn't say him nay: and it was agreed, as they was young, they should wait a year or two. If he and she was of the same mind, he should be free to marry her. Jest right on that, the Captain's regiment was ordered home, and he had to go; and, the next they heard, it was sent off to India. And poor little Ruth she kind o' drooped and pined; but she kept true, and wouldn't have nothin' to say to nobody that came arter her, for there was lots and cords o' fellows as did come arter her. Ye see, Ruth had a takin' way with her; and then she had the name of bein' a great heiress, and that allers draws fellers, as molasses does flies.

"Wal, then the news came, that Captain Oliver was comin' home to England, and the ship was took by the Algerenes, and he was gone into slavery there among them heathen Mahomedans and what not.

"Folks seemed to think it was all over with him, and Ruth might jest as well give up fust as last. And the old Gineral he'd come to think she might do better; and he kep' a introducin' one and another, and tryin' to marry her off; but Ruth she wouldn't. She used to write sheets and sheets to your Aunt Lois about it; and I think Aunt Lois she kep' her grit up. Your Aunt Lois she'd a stuck by a man to the end o' time eft ben her case; and so she told Ruth.

"Wal, then there was young Jeff Sullivan, the Gineral's nephew, he turned up; and the Gineral he took a gret fancy to him. He was next heir to the Gineral; but he'd ben a pretty rackety youngster in his young days, – off to sea, and what not, and sowed a consid'able crop o' wild oats. People said he'd been a pirating off there in South Ameriky. Lordy massy! nobody rightly knew where he hed ben or where he hadn't: all was, he turned up at last all alive, and chipper as a skunk blackbird. Wal, of course he made his court to Ruth; and the Gineral, he rather backed him up in it; but Ruth she wouldn't have nothin' to say to him. Wal, he come and took up his lodgin' at the Gineral's; and he was jest as slippery as an eel, and sort o' slid into every thing, that was a goin' on in the house and about it. He was here, and he was there, and he was everywhere, and a havin' his say about this and that; and he got everybody putty much under his thumb. And they used to say, he wound the Gineral round and round like a skein o' yarn; but he couldn't come it round Ruth.

"Wal, the Gineral said she shouldn't be forced; and Jeff, he was smooth as satin, and said he'd be willing to wait as long as Jacob did for Rachel. And so there he sot down, a watchin' as patient as a cat at a mouse-hole; 'cause the Gineral he was thick-set and short-necked, and drank pretty free, and was one o' the sort that might pop off any time.

"Wal, Mis' Sullivan, she beset the Gineral to make a provision for Ruth; 'cause she told him very sensible, that he'd brought her up in luxury, and that it wa'n't fair not to settle somethin' on her; and so the Gineral he said he'd make a will, and part the property equally between them. And he says to Jeff, that, if he played his part as a young fellow oughter know how, it would all come to him in the end; 'cause they hadn't heard nothing from Captain Oliver for three or four years, and folks about settled it that he must, be dead.

"Wal, the Gineral he got a letter about an estate that had come to him in England; and he had to go over. Wal, livin' on the next estate, was the very cousin of the Gineral's that he was to a married when they was both young: the lands joined so that the grounds run together. What came between them two nobody knows; but she never married, and there she was. There was high words between the Gineral and Madam Sullivan about his goin' over. She said there wa'n't no sort o' need on't, and he said there was; and she said she hoped *she* should be in her grave afore he come back; and he said she might suit herself about that for all him. That 'are was the story that the housekeeper told to Aunt Polly; and Aunt Polly she told me. These 'ere squabbles somehow allers does kind o' leak out one way or t'other. Anyhow, it was a house divided agin itself at the Gineral's, when he was a fixin' out for the voyage. There was Ruth a goin' fust to one, and then to t'other, and tryin' all she could to keep peace beteen 'em; and there was this 'ere Master Slick Tongue talkin' this way to one side, and that way to t'other, and the old Gineral kind o' like a shuttle-cock atween 'em.

"Wal, then, the night afore he sailed, the Gineral he hed his lawyer up in his library there, a lookin' over all his papers and bonds and things, and a witnessing his will; and Master Jeff was there, as lively as a cricket, a goin' into all affairs, and offerin' to take precious good care while he was gone; and the Gineral he had his papers and letters out, a sortin' on 'em over, which was to be took to the old country, and which was to be put in a trunk to go back to Lawyer Dennis's office.

"Wal, Abner Ginger, Polly's boy, he that was footman and waiter then at the Gineral's, he told me, that, about eight o'clock that evening he went up with hot water and lemons and sperits and sich, and he see the gret green table in the library all strewed and covered with piles o' papers; and there was tin boxes a standin' round; and the Gineral a packin' a trunk, and young Master Jeff, as lively and helpful as a rat that smells cheese. And then the Gineral he says, 'Abner,' says he, 'can you write your name?' – 'I should hope so, Gineral.' says Abner. – 'Wal, then, Abner,' says he, 'this is my last will; and I want you to witness it,' and so Abner he put down his name opposite to a place with a wafer and a seal; and then the Gineral, he says, 'Abner, you tell Ginger to come here.' That, you see, was his housekeeper, my Aunt Polly's sister, and a likely woman as ever was. And so they had her up, and she put down her name to the will; and then Aunt Polly she was had up (she was drinking tea there that night), and she put down her name. And all of 'em did it with good heart, 'cause it had got about among 'em that the will was to provide for Miss Ruth; for everybody loved Ruth, ye see, and there was consid'ble many stories kind o' goin' the rounds about Master Jeff and his doin's. And they did say he sort o' kep' up the strife atween the Gineral and my lady, and so they didn't think none too well o' him; and, as he was next o' kin, and Miss Ruth wa'n't none o' the Gineral's blood (ye see, she was Mis'

Sullivan's sister's child), of course there wouldn't nothin' go to Miss Ruth in way o' law, and so that was why the signin' o' that 'are will was so much talked about among 'em."

"Wal, you see, the Gineral he sailed the next day; and Jeff he staid by to keep watch o' things.

"Wal, the old Gineral he got over safe; for Miss Sullivan, she had a letter from him all right. When he got away, his conscience sort o' nagged him, and he was minded to be a good husband. At any rate, he wrote a good loving letter to her, and sent his love to Ruth, and sent over lots o' little keepsakes and things for her, and told her that he left her under good protection, and wanted her to try and make up her mind to marry Jeff, as that would keep the property together.

"Wal, now there couldn't be no sort o' sugar sweeter than Jeff was to them lone wimmen. Jeff was one o' the sort that could be all things to all wimmen. He waited and he tended, and he was as humble as any snake in the grass that ever ye see and the old lady, she clean fell in with him, but Ruth, she seemed to have a regular spite agin him. And she that war as gentle as a lamb, that never had so much as a hard thought of a mortal critter, and wouldn't tread on a worm, she was so set agin Jeff, that she wouldn't so much as touch his hand when she got out o' her kerridge.

"Wal, now comes the strange part o' my story. Ruth was one o' the kind that *hes the gift o' seein'. She was born with a veil over her face!*"

This mysterious piece of physiological information about Ruth was given with a look and air that announced something very profound and awful; and we both took up the inquiry, "Born with a veil over her face? How should *that* make her see?"

"Wal, boys; how should I know? But the fact *is so*. There's those as is wal known as hes the gift o' seein' what others can't see: they can see through walls and houses; they can see people's hearts; they can see what's to come. They don't know nothin' how 'tis, but this 'ere knowledge comes to 'em: it's a gret gift; and that sort's born with the veil over their faces. Ruth was o' these 'ere. Old Granny Badger she was the knowingest old nuss in all these parts; and she was with Ruth's mother when she was born, and she told Lady Lothrop all about it. Says she, 'You may depend upon it that child 'll have the "second-sight"' says she. Oh, that 'are fact was wal known! Wal, that was the reason why Jeff Sullivan couldn't come it round Ruth tho' he was silkier than a milkweed-pod, and jest about as patient as a spider in his hole a watchin' to get his grip on a fly. Ruth wouldn't argue with him, and she wouldn't flout him; but she jest shut herself up in herself, and kept a lookout on him; but she told your Aunt Lois jest what she thought about him.

"Wal, in about six months, come the news that the Gineral was dead. He dropped right down in his tracks, dead with apoplexy, as if he had been shot; and Lady Maxwell she writ a long letter to my lady and Ruth. Ye see, he'd got to be Sir Thomas Sullivan over there; and he was a comin' home to take 'em all over to England to live in grande'r. Wal, my Lady Sullivan (she was then, ye see) she took it drefful hard. Ef they'd a been the lovingest couple in the world, she couldn't a took it harder. Aunt Polly, she said it was all 'cause she thought so much of him, that she fit him so. There's women that thinks so much o' their husbands, that they won't let 'em hev no peace o' their life; and I expect it war so with her, poor soul! Any way, she went right down smack, when she heard he was dead. She was abed, sick, when the news come; and she never spoke nor smiled, jest turned her back to everybody, and kinder wilted and wilted, and was dead in a week. And there was poor little Ruth left all alone in the world, with neither kith nor kin but Jeff.

"Wal, when the funeral was over, and the time app'inted to read the will and settle up matters, there wa'n't no will to be found nowhere, high nor low.

"Lawyer Dean he flew round like a parched pea on a shovel. He said he thought he could a gone in the darkest night, and put his hand on that 'ere will; but when he went where he thought it was, he found it warn't there, and he knowed he'd kep' it under lock and key. What he thought was the will turned out to be an old mortgage. Wal, there was an awful row and a to-do about it, you may be sure. Ruth, she jist said nothin' good or bad. And her not speakin' made Jeff a sight more uncomfortable than ef she'd a hed it out with him. He told her it shouldn't make no sort o' difference; that he should allers stand ready to give her all he hed, if she'd only take him with it. And when it came to that she only gin him a look, and went out o' the room.

"Jeff he flared and flounced and talked, and went round and round a rumpussin' among the papers, but no will was forthcomin', high or low. Wal, now here comes what's remarkable. Ruth she told this 'ere, all the particulars, to yer Aunt Lois and Lady Lothrop. She said that the night after the funeral she went up to her chamber. Ruth had the gret front chamber, opposite to Mis' Sullivan's. I've been in it; it was a monstrous big room, with outlandish furniture in it, that the Gineral brought over from an old palace out to Italy. And there was a great big lookin'-glass over the dressin'-table, that they said come from Venice, that swung so that you could see the whole room in it. Wal, she was a standin' front o' this, jist goin' to undress herself, a hearin' the rain drip on the leaves and the wind a whishin' and whisperin' in the old elm-trees, and jist a thinkin' over her lot, and what should she do now, all alone in the world, when of a sudden she felt a kind o' lightness in her head, and she thought she seemed to see somebody in the glass a movin'. And she looked behind, and there wa'n't nobody there. Then she looked forward in the glass, and saw a strange big room, that she'd never seen before, with a long painted winder in it; and along side o' this stood a tall cabinet with a good many drawers in it. And she saw herself, and knew that it was herself, in this room, along with another woman whose back was turned towards her. She saw herself speak to this woman, and p'int to the cabinet. She saw the woman nod her head. She saw herself go to the cabinet, and open the middle drawer, and take out a bundle o' papers from the very back end on't. She saw her take out a paper from the middle, and open it, and hold it up; and she knew that there was the missin' will. Wal, it all overcome her so that she fainted clean away. And her maid found her a ly-in' front o' the dressin'-table on the floor.

"She was sick of a fever' for a week or fortnight a'ter; and your Aunt Lois she was down takin' care of her; and, as soon as she got able to be moved, she was took out to Lady Lothrop's. Jeff he was jist as attentive and good as he could be; but she wouldn't bear him near her room. If he so much as set a foot on the stairs that led to it she'd know it, and got so wild that he hed to be kept from comin' into the front o' the house. But he was doin' his best to buy up good words from everybody. He paid all the servants double; he kept every one in their places, and did so well by 'em all that the gen'l word among 'em was that Miss Ruth couldn't do better than to marry such a nice, open-handed gentleman.

"Wal, Lady Lothrop she wrote to Lady Maxwell all that hed happened; and Lady

Maxwell, she sent over for Ruth to come over and be a companion for her, and said she'd adopt her, and be as a mother to her.

"Wal, then Ruth she went over with some gentlefolks that was goin' back to England, and offered to see her safe and sound; and so she was set down at Lady Maxwell's manor. It was a grand place, she said, and such as she never see before, – like them old gentry places in England. And Lady Maxwell she made much of her, and cosseted her up for the sake of what the old Gineral had said about her. And Ruth she told her all her story, and how she believed that the will was to be found somewhere, and that she should be led to see it yet.

"She told her, too, that she felt it in her that Cap'n Oliver wasn't dead, and that he'd come back yet. And Lady Maxwell she took up for her with might and main, and said she'd stand by her. But then, ye see, so long as there warn't no will to be found, there warn't nothin' to be done. Jeff was the next heir; and he'd got every thing, stock, and lot, and the estate in England into the bargain. And folks was beginnin' to think putty well of him, as folks allers does when a body is up in the world, and hes houses and lands. Lordy massy! riches allers covers a multitude o' sins.

"Finally, when Ruth hed ben six months with her, one day Lady Maxwell got to tellin' her all about her history, and what hed ben atween her and her cousin, when they was young, and how they hed a quarrel and he flung off to Ameriky, and all them things that it don't do folks no good to remember when it's all over and can't be helped. But she was a lone body, and it seemed to do her good to talk about it.

"Finally, she says to Ruth, says she, 'I'll show you a room in this house you han't seen before. It was the room where we hed that quarrel,' says she; 'and the last I saw of him was there, till he come back to die,' says she.

"So she took a gret key out of her bunch; and she led Ruth along a long passage-way to the other end of the house, and opened on a great library. And the minute Ruth came in, she threw up her hands and gin a great cry. 'Oh!' says she, 'this is the room! and there is the window! and there is the cabinet! and *there in that middle drawer at the back end in a bundle of papers is the will!*

"And Lady Maxwell she said, quite dazed, 'Go look,' says she. And Ruth went, jest as she seed herself do, and opened the drawer, and drew forth from the back part a yellow pile of old letters. And in the middle of those was the will, sure enough. Ruth drew it out, and opened it, and showed it to her.

"Wal, you see that will give Ruth the whole of the Gineral's property in America, tho' it did leave the English estate to Jeff.

"Wal, the end on't was like a story-book.

"Jeff he made believe be mighty glad. And he said it must a ben that the Gineral hed got flustered with the sperit and water, and put that 'ere will in among his letters that he was a doin' up to take back to England. For it was in among Lady Maxwell's letters that she writ him when they was young, and that he'd a kep' all these years and was a takin' back to her.

"Wal, Lawyer Dean said he was sure that Jeff made himself quite busy and useful that night, a tyin' up the papers with red tape, and a packin' the Gineral's trunk; and that, when Jeff gin him his bundle to lock up in his box, he never mistrusted but what he'd got it all right.

"Wal, you see it was jest one of them things that can't be known to the jedgment-day. It might a ben an accident, and then agin it might not; and folks settled it one way or t'other, 'cordin' to their 'pinion o' Jeff; but ye see how 'mazin' handy for him it happened! Why, ef it hadn't ben for the providence I've ben a tellin' about, there it might a lain in them old letters, that Lady Maxwell said she never hed the heart to look over! it never would a turned up in the world."

"Well," said I, "what became of Ruth?" "Oh! Cap'n Oliver he came back all alive, and escaped from the Algerines; and they was married in King's Chapel, and lived in the old Sullivan House, in peace and prosperity. That's jest how the story was; and now Aunt Lois can make what she's a mind ter out on't."

"And what became of Jeff?" "Oh! he started to go over to England, and the ship was wrecked off the Irish coast, and that was the last of him. He never got to his property."

"Good enough for him," said both of us.' "Wal, I don't know: 'twas pretty hard on Jeff. Mebbe he did, and mebbe he didn't. I'm glad I warn't in his shoes, tho'. I'd rather never hed nothin'. This 'ere hastin' to be rich is sich a drefful temptation.

"Wal, now, boys, ye've done a nice lot o' flax, and I guess we'll go up to yer grand'ther's cellar and git a mug o' cyder. Talkin' always gits me dry."

The Minister's Housekeeper

Scene. – The shady side of a blueberry-pasture. – Sam Lawson with the boys, picking blueberries. – Sam, *loq.*

As, you see, boys, 'twas just here, – Parson Carryl's wife, she died along in the forepart o' March: my cousin Huldy, she undertook to keep house for him. The way on't was, that Huldy, she went to take care o' Mis' Carryl in the fust on't, when she fust took sick. Huldy was a tailoress by trade; but then she was one o' these 'ere facultised persons that has a gift for most any thing, and that was how Mis' Carryl come to set sech store by her, that, when she was sick, nothin' would do for her but she must have Huldy round all the time: and the minister, he said he'd make it good to her all the same, and she shouldn't lose nothin' by it. And so Huldy, she staid with Mis' Carryl full three months afore she died, and got to seein' to every thing pretty much round the place.

"Wal, arter Mis' Carryl died, Parson Carryl, he'd got so kind o' used to hevin'

55

on her 'round, takin' care o' things, that he wanted her to stay along a spell; and so Huldy, she staid along a spell, and poured out his tea, and mended his close, and made pies and cakes, and cooked and washed and ironed, and kep' every thing as neat as a pin. Huldy was a drefful chipper sort o' gal; and work sort o' rolled off from her like water off a duck's back. There warn't no gal in Sherburne that could put sich a sight o' work through as Huldy; and yet, Sunday mornin', she always come out in the singers' seat like one o' these 'ere June roses, lookin' so fresh and smilin', and her voice was jest as clear and sweet as a meadow lark's – Lordy massy! I 'member how she used to sing some o' them 'are places where the treble and counter used to go together: her voice kind o' trembled a little, and it sort o' went thro' and thro' a feller! tuck him right where he lived!"

Here Sam leaned contemplatively back with his head in a clump of sweet fern, and refreshed himself with a chew of young wintergreen. "This 'ere young wintergreen, boys, is jest like a feller's thoughts o' things that happened when he was young: it comes up jest so fresh and tender every year, the longest time you hev to live; and you can't help chawin' on't tho' 'tis sort o' stingin'. I don't never get over likin' young wintergreen."

"But about Huldah, Sam?"

"Oh, yes! about Huldy. Lordy massy! when a feller is Indianin' round, these 'ere pleasant summer days, a feller's thoughts gits like a flock o' young partridges: they's up and down and everywhere; 'cause one place is jest about as good as another, when they's all so kind o' comfortable and nice. Wal, about Huldy, – as I was a sayin'. She was jest as handsome a gal to look at as a feller could have; and I think a nice, well-behaved young gal in the singers' seat of a Sunday is a means o' grace: it's sort o' drawin' to the unregenerate, you know. Why, boys, in them days, I've walked ten miles over to Sherburne of a Sunday mornin', jest to play the bass-viol in the same singers' seat with Huldy. She was very much respected, Huldy was; and, when she went out to tailorin', she was allers bespoke six months ahead, and sent for in waggins up and down for ten miles round; for the young fellers was allers 'mazin' anxious to be sent after Huldy, and was quite free to offer to go for her. Wal, after Mis' Carry! died, Huldy got to be sort o' housekeeper at the minister's, and saw to every thing, and did every thing: so that there warn't a pin out o' the way.

"But you know how 'tis in parishes: there allers is women that thinks the minister's affairs belongs to them, and they ought to have the rulin' and guidin' of 'em; and, if a minister's wife dies, there's folks that allers has their eyes open on providences, – lookin' out who's to be the next one.

"Now, there was Mis' Amaziah Pipperidge, a widder with snappin' black eyes, and a hook nose, – kind o' like a hawk; and she was one o' them up-and-down commandin' sort o' women, that feel that they have a call to be seein' to every thing that goes on in the parish, and 'specially to the minister.

"Folks did say that Mis' Pipperidge sort o' sot her eye on the parson for herself:

wal, now that 'are might a been, or it might not. Some folks thought it was a very suitable connection. You see she hed a good property of her own, right nigh to the minister's lot, and was allers kind o' active and busy; so takin' one thing with another, I shouldn't wonder if Mis' Pipperidge should a thought that Providence p'inted that way. At any rate, she went up to Deakin Blod-gett's wife, and they two sort o' put their heads together a mournin' and condolin' about the way things was likely to go on at the minister's now Mis' Carryl was dead. Ye see, the parson's wife, she was one of them women who hed their eyes everywhere and on every thing. She was a little thin woman, but tough as Inger rubber, and smart as a steel trap; and there warn't a hen laid an egg, or cackled, but Mis' Carryl was right there to see about it; and she hed the garden made in the spring, and the medders mowed in summer, and the cider made, and the corn husked, and the apples got in the fall; and the doctor, he hedn't nothin' to do but jest sit stock still a meditatin' on Jerusalem and Jericho and them things that ministers think about.

But Lordy massy! he didn't know nothin' about where any thing he eat or drunk or wore come from or went to: his wife jest led him 'round in temporal things and took care on him like a baby.

"Wal, to be sure, Mis' Carryl looked up to him in spirituals, and thought all the world on him; for there warn't a smarter minister no where 'round. Why, when he preached on decrees and election, they used to come clear over from South Parish, and West Sherburne, and Old Town to hear him; and there was sich a row o' waggins tied along by the meetin'-house that the stables was all full, and all the hitchin'-posts was full clean up to the tavern, so that folks said the doctor made the town look like a gineral trainin'-day a Sunday.

"He was gret on texts, the doctor was. When he hed a p'int to prove, he'd jest go thro' the Bible, and drive all the texts ahead o' him like a flock o' sheep; and then, if there was a text that seemed agin him, why, he'd come out with his Greek and Hebrew, and kind o' chase it 'round a spell, jest as ye see a fellar chase a contrary bell-wether, and make him jump the fence arter the rest. I tell you, there wa'n't no text in the Bible that could stand agin the doctor when his blood was up. The year arter the doctor was app'inted to preach the 'lection sermon in Boston, he made such a figger that the Brattle-street Church sent a committee right down to see if they couldn't get him to Boston; and then the Sherburne folks, they up and raised his salary; ye see, there ain't nothin' wakes folks up like somebody else's wantin' what you've got. Wal, that fall they made him a Doctor o' Divinity at Cambridge College, and so they sot more by him than ever. Wal, you see, the doctor, of course he felt kind o' lonesome and afflicted when Mis' Carryl was gone; but railly and truly, Huldy was so up to every thing about house, that the doctor didn't miss nothin' in a temporal way. His shirt-bosoms was pleated finer than they ever was, and them ruffles 'round his wrists was kep' like the driven snow; and there warn't a brack in his silk stockin's, and his shoe buckles was kep' polished up, and his coats brushed; and then there warn't no bread and biscuit like Huldy's; and her butter was like solid lumps o' gold; and there wern't no pies to equal hers; and so the doctor never felt the loss o' Miss Carryl at table. Then there was Huldy allers opposite to him, with her blue eyes and her cheeks like two fresh peaches. She was kind o' pleasant to look at; and the more the doctor looked at her the better he liked her; and so things seemed to be goin' on quite quiet and comfortable ef it hadn't been that Mis' Pipperidge and Mis' Deakin Blodgett and Mis' Sawin got their heads together a talkin' about things.

"'Poor man,' says Mis' Pipperidge, 'what can that child that he's got there do towards takin' the care of all that place? It takes a mature woman,' she says, 'to tread in Mis' Carryl's shoes.'

"'That it does,' said Mis' Blodgett; and, when things once get to runnin' down hill, there ain't no stoppin' on 'em,' says she.

"Then Mis' Sawin she took it up. (Ye see, Mis' Sawin used to go out to dress-makin', and was sort o' 'jealous, 'cause folks sot more by Huldy than they did by her). 'Well,' says she, 'Huldy Peters is well enough at her trade. I never denied that, though I do say I never did believe in her way o' makin' button-holes; and I must say, if 'twas the dearest friend I hed, that I thought Huldy tryin' to fit Mis' Kit-tridge's plumb-colored silk was a clear piece o' presumption; the silk was jist spiled, so 'twarn't fit to come into the meetin'-house. I must say, Huldy's a gal that's always too ventersome about takin' 'spon-sibilities she don't know nothin' about.'

"'Of course she don't,' said Mis' Deakin Blodgett. 'What does she know about all the lookin' and see-in' to that there ought to be in guidin' the minister's house. Huldy's well meanin', and she's good at her work, and good in the singers' seat; but Lordy massy! she hain't got no experience. Parson Carryl ought to have an experienced woman to keep house for him. There's the spring house-cleanin' and the fall house-cleanin' to be seen to, and the things to be put away from the moths; and then the gettin' ready for the association and all the ministers' meetin's; and the makin' the soap and the candles, and settin' the hens and turkeys, watchin' the calves, and seein' after the hired men and the garden; and there that 'are blessed man jist sets there at home as serene, and has nobody 'round but that 'are gal, and don't even know how things must be a runnin' to waste!'

"Wal, the upshot on't was, they fussed and fuzzled and wuzzled till they'd drinked up all the tea in the teapot; and then they went down and called on the parson, and wuzzled him all up talkin' about this, that, and t'other that wanted lookin' to, and that it was no way to leave every thing to a young chit like Huldy, and that he ought to be lookin' about for an experienced woman. The parson he thanked 'em kindly, and said he believed their motives was good, but he didn't go no further. He didn't ask Mis' Pipperidge to come and stay there and help him, nor nothin' o' that kind; but he said he'd attend to matters himself. The fact was, the parson had got such a likin' for havin' Huldy 'round, that he couldn't think o' such a thing as swappin' her off for the Widder Pipperidge.

"But he thought to himself, 'Huldy is a good girl; but I oughtn't to be a leavin' every thing to her, – it's too hard on her. I ought to be instructin' and guidin' and helpin' of her; 'cause 'tain't everybody could be expected to know and do what Mis' Carryl did;' and so at it he went; and Lordy massy! didn't Huldy hev a time on't when the minister began to come out of his study, and want to tew 'round and see to things? Huldy, you see, thought all the world of the minister, and she was 'most afraid to laugh; but she told me she couldn't, for the life of her, help it when his back was turned, for he wuzzled things up in the most singular way. But Huldy she'd jest say 'Yes, sir,' and get him off into his study, and go on her own way.

"'Huldy,' says the minister one day, 'you ain't experienced out doors; and, when you want to know any thing, you must come to me.'

"'Yes, sir,' says Huldy.

"'Now, Huldy,' says the parson, 'you must be sure to save the turkey-eggs, so that we can have a lot of turkeys for Thanksgiving.'

"'Yes, sir,' says Huldy; and she opened the pantry-door, and showed him a nice dishful she'd been a savin' up. Wal, the very next day the parson's hen-turkey was found killed up to old Jim Scroggs's barn. Folks said Scroggs killed it; though Scroggs, he stood to it he didn't: at any rate, the Scroggses, they made a meal on't; and Huldy, she felt bad about it 'cause she'd set her heart on raisin' the turkeys; and says she, 'Oh, dear! I don't know what I shall do. I was just ready to see [set] her.'

"'Do, Huldy?' says the parson: 'why, there's the other turkey, out there by the door; and a fine bird, too, he is.' Sure enough, there was the old tom-turkey a struttin' and a sidlin' and a quitterin,' and a floutin' his tail-feathers in the sun, like a lively young widower, all ready to begin life over agin.

"'But,' says Huldy, 'you know he can't set on eggs.'

"'He can't? I'd like to know why,' says the parson. 'He 'shall' set on eggs, and hatch 'em too.'

"'O doctor!' says Huldy, all in a tremble; 'cause, you know, she didn't want to contradict the minister, and she was afraid she should laugh, – 'I never heard that a tom-turkey would set on eggs.'

"'Why, they ought to,' said the parson, getting quite 'arnest: 'what else be they good for? you just bring out the eggs, now, and put 'em in the nest, and I'll make him set on 'em.'

"So Huldy she thought there wern't no way to convince him but to let him try: so she took the eggs out, and fixed 'em all nice in the nest; and then she come back and found old Tom a skirmishin' with the parson pretty lively, I tell ye. Ye see, old Tom he didn't take the idee at all; and he flopped and gobbled, and fit the parson; and the parson's wig got 'round so that his cue stuck straight out over his ear, but he'd got his blood up. Ye see, the old doctor was used to carryin' his p'ints o' doctrine; and he hadn't fit the Arminians and Socinians to be beat by a tom-turkey;

so finally he made a dive, and ketched him by the neck in spite o' his floppin', and stroked him down, and put Huldy's apron 'round him.

"'There, Huldy,' he says, quite red in the face, 'we've got him now; 'and he travelled off to the barn with him as lively as a cricket.

"Huldy came behind jist chokin' with laugh, and afraid the minister would look 'round and see her.

"'Now, Huldy, we'll crook his legs, and set him down,' says the parson, when they got him to the nest: 'you see he is getting quiet, and he'll set there all right.'

"And the parson, he sot him down; and old Tom he sot there solemn enough, and held his head down all droopin', lookin' like a rail pious old cock, as long as the parson sot by him.

"'There: you see how still he sets,' says the parson to Huldy.

"Huldy was 'most dyin' for fear she should laugh. 'I'm afraid he'll get up,' says she, 'when you do.'

"'Oh, no, he won't!' says the parson, quite confident. 'There, there,' says he, layin' his hands on him, as if pronouncin' a blessin'. But when the parson riz up, old Tom he riz up too, and began to march over the eggs.

"'Stop, now!' says the parson. 'I'll make him get down agin: hand me that corn-basket; we'll put that over him.'

"So he crooked old Tom's legs, and got him down agin; and they put the corn-basket over him, and then they both stood and waited.

"'That'll do the thing, Huldy,' said the parson.

"'I don't know about it,' says Huldy.

"'Oh, yes, it will, child! I understand,' says he.

"Just as he spoke, the basket riz right up and stood, and they could see old Tom's long legs.

"'I'll make him stay down, confound him,' says the parson; for, ye see, parsons is men, like the rest on us, and the doctor had got his spunk up.

"'You jist hold him a minute, and I'll get something that'll make him stay, I guess;' and out he went to the fence, and brought in a long, thin, flat stone, and laid it on old Tom's back.

"Old Tom he wilted down considerable under this, and looked railly as if he was goin' to give in. He staid still there a good long spell, and the minister and Huldy left him there and come up to the house; but they hadn't more than got in the door before they see old Tom a hippin' along, as high-steppin' as ever, sayin' 'Talk! talk! and quitter! quitter!' and struttin' and gobblin' as if he'd come through the Red Sea, and got the victory.

"'Oh, my eggs!' says Huldy. 'I'm afraid he's smashed 'em!'

"And sure enough, there they was, smashed flat enough under the stone.

"'I'll have him killed,' said the parson: 'we won't have such a critter 'round.'

"But the parson, he slep' on't, and then didn't do it: he only come out next Sunday with a tip-top sermon on the 'Riginal Cuss' that was pronounced on things in gineral, when Adam fell, and showed how every thing was allowed to go contrary ever since. There was pig-weed, and pusley, and Canady thistles, cut-worms, and bag-worms, and canker-worms, to say nothin' of rattlesnakes. The doctor made it very impressive and sort o' improvin'; but Huldy, she told me, goin' home, that she hardly could keep from laughin' two or three times in the sermon when she thought of old Tom a standin' up with the corn-basket on his back.

"Wal, next week Huldy she jist borrowed the minister's horse and side-saddle, and rode over to South Parish to her Aunt Bascome's, – Widder Bascome's, you know, that lives there by the trout-brook, – and got a lot o' turkey-eggs o' her, and come back and set a hen on 'em, and said nothin'; and in good time there was as nice a lot o' turkey-chicks as ever ye see.

"Huldy never said a word to the minister

about his experiment, and he never said a word to her; but he sort o' kep' more to his books, and didn't take it on him to advise her.

"But not long arter he took it into his head that Huldy ought to have a pig to be a fattin' with the buttermilk. Mis' Pipperidge set him up to it; and jist then old Tim Bigelow, out to Juniper Hill, told him if he'd call over he'd give him a little pig.

"So he sent for a man, and told him to build a pigpen right out by the well, and have it all ready when he came home with his pig.

"Huldy she said she wished he might put a curb round the well out there, because in the dark, sometimes, a body might stumble into it; and the parson, he told him he might do that.

"Wal, old Aikin, the carpenter, he didn't come till most the middle of the arternoon; and then he sort o' idled, so that he didn't get up the well-curb till sundown; and then he went off and said he'd come and do the pig-pen next day.

"Wal, arter dark, Parson Carryl he driv into the yard, full chizel, with his pig. He'd tied up his mouth to keep him from squeelin'; and he see what he thought was the pig-pen, – he was rather nearsighted, – and so he ran and threw piggy over; and down he dropped into the water, and the minister put out his horse and pranced off into the house quite delighted.

"'There, Huldy, I've got you a nice little pig.'

"'Dear me!' says Huldy: 'where have you put him?'

"'Why, out there in the pig-pen, to be sure.'

"'Oh, dear me!' says Huldy: 'that's the well-curb; there ain't no pig-pen built,' says she.

"'Lordy massy!' says the parson: 'then I've thrown the pig in the well!'

"Wal, Huldy she worked and worked, and finally she fished piggy out in the bucket, but he was dead as a door-nail; and she got him out o' the way quietly, and didn't say much; and the parson, he took to a great Hebrew book in his study; and says he, 'Huldy, I ain't much in temporals,' says he. Huldy says she kind o' felt her heart go out to him, he was so sort o' meek and helpless and lamed; and says she, 'Wal, Parson Carryl, don't trouble your head no more about it; I'll see to things;' and sure enough, a week arter there was a nice pen, all ship-shape, and two little white pigs that Huldy bought with the money for the butter she sold at the store.

"'Wal, Huldy,' said the parson, 'you are a most amazin' child: you don't say nothin' but you do more than most folks.'

"Arter that the parson set sich store by Huldy that he come to her and asked her about every thing, and it was amazin' how every thing she put her hand to prospered. Huldy planted marigolds and larkspurs, pinks and carnations, all up and down the path to the front door, and trained up mornin' glories and scarlet-runners round the windows. And she was always a gettin' a root here, and a sprig there, and a seed from somebody else: for Huldy was one o' them that has the gift, so that ef you jist give 'em the leastest sprig of any thing they make a great bush out of it right away; so that in six months Huldy had roses and geraniums and lilies, sich as it would a took a gardener to raise. The parson, he took no notice at fust; but when the yard was all ablaze with flowers he used to come and stand in a kind o' maze at the front door, and say, 'Beautiful, beautiful: why, Huldy, I never see any thing like it.' And then when her work was done arternoons, Huldy would sit with her sewin' in the porch, and sing and trill away till she'd draw the meadow-larks and the bobolinks, and the orioles to answer her, and the great big elm-tree overhead would get perfectly rackety with the birds; and the parson, settin' there in his study, would git to kind o' dreamin' about the angels, and golden harps, and the New Jerusalem; but he wouldn't speak a word, 'cause Huldy she was jist like them wood-thrushes, she never could sing so well when she thought folks was hearin'. Folks noticed, about this time, that the parson's sermons got to be like Aaron's rod, that budded and blossomed: there was things in 'em about flowers and birds, and more 'special about the music o' heaven. And Huldy she noticed, that ef there was a hymn run in her head while she was 'round a workin' the minister was sure to give it out next Sunday. You see, Huldy was jist like a bee: she always sung when she was workin', and you could hear her trillin', now down in the corn-patch, while she was pickin' the corn; and now in the buttery, while she was workin' the butter; and now she'd go singin' down cellar, and then she'd be singin' up over head, so that she seemed to fill a house chock full o' music.

"Huldy was so sort o' chipper and fair spoken, that she got the hired men all under her thumb: they come to her and took her orders jist as meek as so many calves; and she traded at the store, and kep' the accounts, and she hed her eyes everywhere, and tied up all the ends so tight that there want no gettin' 'round her. She wouldn't let nobody put nothin' off on Parson Carryl, 'cause he was a minister. Huldy was allers up to anybody that wanted to make a hard bargain; and, afore he knew jist what he was about, she'd got the best end of it, and everybody said that Huldy was the most capable gal that they'd ever traded with.

"Wal, come to the meetin' of the Association, Mis' Deakin Blodgett and Mis' Pipperidge come callin' up to the parson's, all in a stew, and offerin' their services to get the house ready; but the doctor, he jist thanked 'em quite quiet, and turned 'em over to Huldy; and Huldy she told 'em that she'd got every thing ready, and showed 'em her pantries, and her cakes and her pies and her puddin's, and took 'em all over the house; and they went peekin' and pokin', openin' cupboard-doors, and lookin' into drawers; and they couldn't find so much as a thread out o' the way, from garret to cellar, and so they went off quite discontented. Arter that the women set a new trouble a brewin'. Then they begun to talk that it was a year now since Mis' Carryl died; and it r'ally wasn't proper such a young gal to be stayin' there, who everybody could see was a settin' her cap for the minister.

"Mis' Pipperidge said, that, so long as she looked on Huldy as the hired gal, she hadn't thought much about it; but

Huldy was railly takin' on airs as an equal, and appearin' as mistress o' the house in a way that would make talk if it went on. And Mis' Pipperidge she driv 'round up to Deakin Abner Snow's, and down to Mis' 'Lijah Perry's, and asked them if they wasn't afraid that the way the parson and Huldy was a goin' on might make talk. And they said they hadn't thought on't before, but now, come to think on't, they was sure it would; and they all went and talked with somebody else, and asked them if they didn't think it would make talk. So come Sunday, between meetin's there warn't noth-in' else talked about; and Huldy saw folks a noddin' and a winkin', and a lookin' arter her, and she begun to feel drefful sort o' disagreeable. Finally Mis' Sawin she says to her, 'My dear, didn't you, never think folk would talk about you and the minister?'

"'No: why should they?' says Huldy, quite innocent.

"Wal, dear,' says she, 'I think it's a shame; but they say you're tryin' to catch him, and that it's so bold and improper for you to be courtin' of him right in his own house, – you know folks will talk, – I thought I'd tell you 'cause I think so much of you,' says she.

"Huldy was a gal of spirit, and she despised the talk, but it made her drefful uncomfortable; and when she got home at night she sat down in the mornin'-glory porch, quite quiet, and didn't sing a word.

"The minister he had heard the same thing from one of his deakins that day; and, when he saw Huldy so kind o' silent, he says to her, 'Why don't you sing, my child?'

"He hed a pleasant sort o' way with him, the minister had, and Huldy had got to likin' to be with him; and it all come over her that perhaps she ought to go away; and her throat kind o' filled up so she couldn't hardly speak; and, says she, 'I can't sing to-night.'

"Says he, 'You don't know how much good you're singin' has done me, nor how much good *you* have done me in all ways, Huldy. I wish I knew how to show my gratitude.'

"'O sir!' says Huldy, '*is* it improper for me to be here?'

"'No, dear,' says the minister, 'but ill-natured folks will talk; but there is one way we can stop it, Huldy – if you will marry me. You'll make me very happy, and I'll do all I can to make you happy. Will you?'

"Wal, Huldy never told me jist what she said to the minister, – gals never does give you the particulars of them 'are things jist as you'd like 'em, – only I know the upshot and the hull on't was, that Huldy she did a consid'able lot o' clear starchin' and ironin' the next two days; and the Friday o' next week the minister and she rode over together to Dr. Lothrop's in Old Town; and the doctor, he jist made 'em man and wife, 'spite of envy of the Jews,' as the hymn says. Wal, you'd better believe there was a starin' and a wonderin' next Sunday mornin' when the second bell was a tollin', and the minister walked up the broad aisle with Huldy, all in white, arm in arm with him, and he opened the minister's pew, and handed her in as if she was a princess; for, you see, Parson Carryl come of a good family, and was a born gentleman, and had a sort o' grand way o' bein' polite to women-folks. Wal, I guess there was a rus'lin' among the bunnets. Mis' Pipperidge gin a great bounce, like corn poppin' on a shovel, and her eyes glared through her glasses at Huldy as if they'd a sot her afire; and everybody in the meetin' house was a starin', I tell *yew*. But they couldn't none of 'em say nothin' agin Huldy's looks; for there wa'n't a crimp nor a frill about her that wa'n't jis' *so*; and her frock was white as the driven snow, and she had her bunnet all trimmed up with white ribbins; and all the fellows said the old doctor had stole a march, and got the handsomest gal in the parish.

"Wal, arter meetin' they all come 'round the parson and Huldy at the door, shakin' hands and laugh-in'; for by that time they was about agreed that they'd got to let putty well alone.

"'Why, Parson Carryl,' says Mis' Deakin Blod-gett, 'how you've come it over us.'

"'Yes,' says the parson, with a kind o' twinkle in his eye. 'I thought,' says he, 'as folks wanted to talk about Huldy and me, I'd give 'em somethin' wuth talkin' about.'"

The Widow's Bandbox

"Lordy massy! Stick yer hat into the nor'east, Horace, and see 'f ye can't stop out this 'ere wind. I'm e'eny most used up with it." So spake Sam Lawson, contemplating mournfully a new broad-brimmed straw hat in which my soul was rejoicing. It was the dripping end of a sour November afternoon, which closed up a "spell o' weather" that had been steadily driving wind and rain for a week past; and we boys sought the shelter and solace of his shop, and, opening the door, let in the wind aforesaid.

Sam had been all day in one of his periodical fits of desperate industry. The smoke and sparks had been seen flying out of his shop-chimney in a frantic manner; and the blows of his hammer had resounded with a sort of feverish persistence, intermingled with a doleful wailing of psalm-tunes of the most lugubrious description.

These fits of industry on Sam's part were an affliction to us boys, especially when they happened to come on

Saturday: for Sam was as much a part of our Saturday-afternoon calculations as if we had a regular deed of property in him; and we had been all day hanging round his shop, looking in from time to time, in the vague hope that he would propose something to brighten up the dreary monotony of a holiday in which it had been impossible to go anywhere or do any thing.

"Sam, ain't you coming over to tell us some stories to-night?"

"Bless your soul and body, boys! life ain't made to be spent tellin' stories. Why, I shall hev to be up here workin' till arter twelve o'clock," said Sam, who was suddenly possessed with a spirit of the most austere diligence. "Here I be up to my neck in work, – things kind o' comin' in a heap together. There's Mis' Cap'n Broad's andirons, she sent word she must have 'em to-night; and there's Lady Lothrop, she wants her warmin'-pan right off; they can't non' on 'em wait a minit longer. I've ben a drivin' and workin' all day like a nigger-slave. Then there was Jeduth Pettybone, he brought down them colts to-day, and I worked the biggest part o' the mornin' shoein' on 'em; and then Jeduth he said he couldn't make change to pay me, so there wa'n't nothin' comin' in for 't; and then Hepsy she kep' a jawin' at me all dinner-time 'bout that. Why, I warn't to blame now, was I? I can't make everybody do jest right and pay regular, can I? So ye see it goes, boys, gettin' yer bread by the sweat o' your brow; and sometimes sweatin' and not gettin' yer bread. That 'ere's what I call the *cuss*, the 'riginal cuss, that come on man for hearkenin' to the voice o' his wife, – that 'ere was what did it. It allers kind o' riles me up with Mother Eve when I think on't. The women hain't no bisness to fret as they do, 'cause they sot this 'ere state o' things goin' in the fust place."

"But, Sam, Aunt Lois and Aunt Nabby are both going over to Mis'. Mehitabel's to tea. Now, you just come over and eat supper with us and tell us a story, do."

"Gone out to tea, be they?" said Sam, relaxing his hammering, with a brightening gleam stealing gradually across his lanky visage. "Wal, that 'ere looks like a providential openin', to be sure. Wal, I guess I'll come. What's the use o' never havin' a good time? Ef you work yourself up into shoestrings you don't get no thanks for it, and things in this world's 'bout as broad as they is long: the women 'll scold, turn 'em which way ye will. A good mug o' cider and some cold victuals over to the Deakin's 'll kind o' comfort a feller up; and your granny she's sort o' merciful, she don't rub it into a fellow all the time like Miss Lois."

"Now, let's see, boys," said Sam, when a comfortable meal of pork and beans had been disposed of, and a mug of cider was set down before the fire to warm. "I s'pect ye'll like to hear a Down-East story to-night."

Of course we did, and tumbled over each other in our eagerness to get the nearest place to the narrator.

Sam's method of telling a story was as leisurely as that of some modern novelwriters. He would take his time for it, and proceed by easy stages. It was like the course of a dreamy, slow-moving river through a tangled meadow-flat, —

not a rush nor a bush but was reflected in it; in short, Sam gave his philosophy of matters and things in general as he went along, and was especially careful to impress an edifying moral.

"Wal, ye see, boys, ye know I was born down to Newport, – there where it's all ships and shipping, and sich. My old mother she kep' a boardin'-house for sailors down there. Wal, ye see, I rolled and tumbled round the world pretty consid'able afore I got settled down here in Oldtown.

"Ye see, my mother she wanted to bind me out to a blacksmith, but I kind o' sort o' didn't seem to take to it. It was kind o' hard work, and boys is apt to want to take life easy. Wal, I used to run off to the sea-shore, and lie stretched out on them rocks there, and look off on to the water; and it did use to look so sort o' blue and peaceful, and the ships come a sailin' in and out so sort o' easy and natural, that I felt as if that are'd be jest the easiest kind o' life a fellow could have. All he had to do was to get aboard one o' them ships, and be off seekin' his fortin at t'other end o' the rainbow, where gold grows on bushes and there's valleys o' diamonds.

"So, nothin' would do but I gin my old mother the slip; and away I went to sea, with my duds tied up in a han'kercher.

"I tell ye what, boys, ef ye want to find an easy life, don't ye never go to sea. I tell ye, life on shipboard ain't what it looks to be on shore. I hadn't been aboard more'n three hours afore I was the sickest critter that ever ye did see; and I tell you, I didn't get no kind o' compassion. Cap'ns and mates they allers thinks boys hain't no kind o' business to have no bowels nor nothin', and they put it on 'em sick or well. It's jest a kick here, and a cuff there, and a twitch by the ear in t'other place; one a shovin' on 'em this way, and another hittin' on 'em a clip, and all growlin' from mornin' to night. I believe the way my ears got so long was bein' hauled out o' my berth by 'em: that 'are's a sailor's regular way o' wakin' up a boy.

"Wal, by time I got to the Penobscot country, all I wanted to know was how to get back agin. That 'are's jest the way folks go all their lives, boys. It's all fuss, fuss, and stew, stew, till ye get somewhere; and then it's fuss, fuss, and stew, stew, to get back agin; jump here and scratch yer eyes out, and jump there and scratch 'em in agin, – that 'are's life.

"Wal, I kind o' poked round in Penobscot country till I got a berth on 'The Brilliant' that was lyin' at Camden, goin' to sail to Boston.

"Ye see, 'The Brilliant' she was a tight little sloop in the government service: 'twas in the war-times, ye see, and Commodore Tucker that is now (he was Cap'n Tucker then), he had the command on her, – used to run up and down all the coast takin' observations o' the British, and keepin' his eye out on 'em, and givin' on 'em a nip here and a clip there,' cordin' as he got a good chance. Why, your grand'ther knew old Commodore Tucker. It was he that took Dr. Franklin over Minister, to France, and dodged all the British vessels, right in the middle o' the war. I tell you that 'are was like runnin' through the drops in a thunder-shower. He got chased by the British ships pretty consid'able, but he was too spry for 'em. Arter the war was over, Commodore Tucker took over John Adams, our fust Minister to England. A drefful smart man the Commodore was, but he most like to 'a' ben took in this 'ere time I'm a tellin' ye about, and all 'cause he was sort o' softhearted to the women. Tom Toothacre told me the story. Tom he was the one that got me the berth on the ship. Ye see, I used to know Tom at Newport; and once when he took sick there my mother nussed him up, and that was why Tom was friends with me and got me the berth, and kep' me warm in it too. Tom he was one of your rael Maine boys, that's hatched out, so to speak, in water like ducks. He was born away down there on Harpswell P'int; and they say, if ye throw one o' them Harpswell babies into the sea, he'll take to it nateral, and swim like a cork: ef they hit their heads agin a rock it only dents the rock, but don't hurt the baby. Tom he was a great character on the ship. He could see farther, and knew more 'bout wind and water, than most folks: the officers took Tom's judgment, and the men all went by his say. My mother she chalked a streak o' good luck for me when she nussed up Tom.

"Wal, we wus a lyin' at Camden there, one arternoon, goin' to sail for Boston that night. It was a sort o' soft, pleasant arternoon, kind o' still, and there wa'n't nothin' a goin' on but jest the hens a craw-crawin', and a histin' up one foot, and holdin' it a spell 'cause they didn't know when to set it down, and the geese a sissin' and a pickin' at the grass. Ye see, Camden wasn't nothin' of a place, – 'twas jest as if somebody had emptied out a pocketful o' houses and forgot 'em. There wer'n't nothin' a stirrin' or goin' on; and so we was all took aback, when 'bout four o'clock in the arternoon there come a boat alongside, with a tall, elegant lady in it, all dressed in deep mournin'. She rared up sort o' princess-like, and come aboard our ship, and wanted to speak to Cap'n Tucker. Where she come from, or what she wanted, or where she was goin' to, we none on us knew: she kep' her veil down so we couldn't get sight o' her face. All was, she must see Cap'n Tucker alone right away.

"Wal, Cap'n Tucker he was like the generality o' cap'ns. He was up to 'bout every thing that any *man* could do, but it was pretty easy for a woman to come it over him. Ye see, cap'ns, they don't see women as men do ashore. They don't have enough of 'em to get tired on 'em; and every woman's an angel to a sea-cap'n. Anyway, the cap'n he took her into his cabin, and he sot her a chair, and was her humble servant to command, and what would she have of him? And we was all a winkin', and a nudgin' each other, and a peekin' to see what was to come o' it. And she see it; and so she asks, in a sort o' princess' way, to speak to the cap'n alone; and so the doors was shut, and we was left to our own ideas, and a wonderin' what it was all to be about.

"Wal, you see, it come out arterwards all about what went on; and things went this way. Jest as soon as the doors was shut, and she was left alone with the cap'n, she busted out a cryin' and a sobbin' fit to break her heart.

"Wal, the cap'n he tried to comfort her up: but no, she wouldn't be comforted, but went on a weepin' and a wailin,' and a wringin' on her hands, till the poor cap'n's heart was a'most broke; for the cap'n was the tenderest-hearted critter that could be, and couldn't bear to see a child or a woman in trouble noways.

"'O cap'n!' said she, 'I'm the most unfortunate woman. I'm all alone in the world,' says she, 'and I don't know what'll become of me ef you don't keep me,' says she.

"Wal, the cap'n thought it was time to run up his colors; and so says he, 'Ma'am, I'm a married man, and love my wife,' says he, 'and so I can feel for all women in distress,' says he.

"Oh, well, then!' says she,'you can feel for me, and know how to pity me. My dear husband's just died suddenly when he was up the river. He was took with the fever in the woods. I nussed him day and night,' says she; 'but he died there in a mis'able little hut far from home and friends,' says she; 'and I've brought his body down with me, hopin' Providence would open some way to get it back to our home in Boston. And now, cap'n, you must help me.'

"Then the cap'n see what she was up to: and he hated to do it, and tried to cut her off o' askin'; but she wa'n't to be put off.

"'Now, cap'n,' says she, 'ef you'll take me and the body o' my husband on board to-night, I'd be willin' to reward you to any amount. Money would be no object to me,' says she.

"Wal, you see, the cap'n he kind o' hated to do it; and he hemmed and hawed, and he tried to 'pologize. He said 'twas a government vessel, and he didn't know as he had a right to use it. He said sailors was apt to be superstitious; and he didn't want 'em to know as there was a corpse on board.

"'Wal,' says she, 'why need they know? 'For, you see, she was up to every dodge; and she said she'd come along with it at dusk, in a box, and have it just carried to a state-room, and he needn't tell nobody what it was.

"Wal, Cap'n Tucker he hung off; and he tried his best to persuade her to have a funeral, all quiet, there at Camden. He promised to get a minister, and 'tend to it, and wait a day till it was all over, and then take her on to Boston free gratis. But 'twas all no go. She wouldn't hear a word to 't. And she reeled off the talk to him by the yard. And, when talk failed, she took to her water-works again, till finally the cap'n said his resolution was clean washed away, and he jest give up hook and line; and so 'twas all settled and arranged, that, when evening come, she was to be alongside with her boat, and took aboard.

"When she come out o' the cap'n's room to go off, I see Tom Toothacre a watchin' on her. He stood there by the railin's a shavin' up a plug o' baccy to put in his pipe. He didn't say a word; but he sort o' took the measure o' that 'are woman with his eye, and kept a follerin' on her.

"She had a fine sort o' lively look, carried her head up and shoulders back, and stepped as if she had steel springs in her heels.

"'Wal, Tom, what do ye say to her?' says Ben Bowdin.

"'I don't *say* nothin',' says Tom, and he lit his pipe; 'tain't *my* busness,' says he.

"'Wal, what do you *think?*' says Ben. Tom gin a hist to his trousers.

"'My thoughts is my own,' says he; 'and I calculate to keep 'em to myself,' says he. And then he jest walked to the side of the vessel, and watched the woman a gettin' ashore. There was a queer kind o' look in Tom's eye.

"Wal, the cap'n he was drefful sort o' oneasy arter she was gone. He had a long talk in the cabin with Mr. More, the fust officer; and there was a sort o' stir aboard as if somethin' was a goin' to happen, we couldn't jest say what it was.

"Sometimes it seems as if, when things is goin' to happen, a body kind o' feels 'em comin' in the air. We boys was all that way: o' course we didn't know nothin' 'bout what the woman wanted, or what she come for, or whether she was comin' agin; 'n fact, we didn't know nothin' about it, and yet we sort o' expected suthin' to come o' it; and suthin' did come, sure enough.

"Come on night, jest at dusk, we see a boat comin' alongside; and there, sure enough, was the lady in it.

"'There, she's comin' agin,' says I to Tom Tooth-acre.

"'Yes, and brought her baggage with her,' says Tom; and he p'inted down to a long, narrow pine box that was in the boat beside her.

"Jest then the cap'n called on Mr. More, and he called on Tom Toothacre; and among 'em they lowered a tackle, and swung the box aboard, and put it in the state-room right alongside the cap'n's cabin.

"The lady she thanked the cap'n and Mr. More, and her voice was jest as sweet as any nightingale; and she went into the state-room arter they put the body in, and was gone ever so long with it. The cap'n and Mr. More they stood a whisperin' to each other, and every once in a while they'd kind o' nod at the door where the lady was.

"Wal, by and by she come out with her han'ker-chief to her eyes, and come on deck, and begun talk-in' to the cap'n and Mr. More, and a wishin' all kinds o' blessin's on their heads.

"Wal, Tom Toothacre didn't say a word, good or bad; but he jest kep' a lookin' at her, watchin' her as a cat watches a mouse. Finally we up sail, and started with a fair breeze. The lady she kep' a walkin' up and down, up and down, and every time she turned on her heel, I saw Tom a lookin' arter her and kind o' noddin' to himself.

"'What makes you look arter her so, Tom?' says I to him.

"'Cause I think she *wants* lookin' arter,' says Tom. 'What's more,' says he, 'if the cap'n don't look sharp arter her the devil 'll have us all afore mornin.' I tell ye, Sam, there's mischief under them petticuts.'

"'Why, what do ye think?' says I.

"'Think! I don't think, I knows! That 'are's no gal, nor widder neither, if my name's Tom Tooth-acre! Look at her walk; look at the way she turns on her heel I I've been a watchin' on her. There ain't no woman livin' with a step like that!' says he.

"'Wal, who should the critter be, then?' says I.

"'Wal,' says Tom, 'ef that 'are ain't a British naval officer, I lose my bet. I've been used to the ways on 'em, and I knows their build and their step.'

"'And what do you suppose she's got in that long box?' says I.

"'What has she got?' says Tom. 'Wal, folks might say none o' my bisness; but I s'pects it'll turn out some o' my bisness, and yourn too, if he don't look sharp arter it,' says Tom. 'It's no good, that 'are box ain't.'

"'Why don't you speak to Mr. More?' says I.

"'Wal, you see she's a chipperin' round and a mak-in' herself agreeable to both on 'em, you see; she don't mean to give nobody any chance for a talk with 'em; but I've got my eye on her, for all that. You see I hain't no sort o' disposition to sarve out a time on one o' them British prison-ships,' says Tom Toothacre. 'It might be almighty handy for them British to have "The Brilliant" for a coast-vessel,' says he; 'but, ye see, it can't be spared jest yet. So, madam,' says he,'I've got my eye on you.'

"Wal, Tom was as good as his word; for when Mr. More came towards him at the wheel, Tom he up and says to him, 'Mr. More,' says he, 'that 'are big box in the state-room yonder wants lookin' into.'

"Tom was a sort o' privileged character, and had a way o' speakin' up that the officers took in good part, 'cause they knew he was a fust-rate hand.

"Wal, Mr. More he looks mysterious; and says he, Tom, do the boys know what's in that 'are box?'

"'I bet they don't,' says Tom. 'If they had, you wouldn't a got 'em to help it aboard.'

"'Wal, you see, poor woman,' says Mr. More to Tom, 'she was so distressed. She wanted to get her husband's body to Boston; and there wa'n't no other way, and so the cap'n let it come aboard. He didn't want the boys to suspect what it really Was.'

"'Husband's body be hanged!' said Tom. 'Guess that 'are corpse ain't so dead but what there'll be a resurrection afore mornin', if it ain't looked arter,' says he.

"'Why, what do you mean, Tom?' said Mr. More, all in a blue maze.

"'I mean, that 'are gal that's ben a switchin' her petticuts up and down our deck ain't no gal at all. That are's a British officer, Mr. More. You give my duty to the cap'n, and tell him to look into his wid-der's bandbox, and see what he'll find there.'

"Wal, the mate he went and had a talk with the cap'n; and they 'greed between 'em that Mr. More was to hold her in talk while the cap'n went and took observations in the state-room.

"So, down the cap'n goes into the state-room to give a look at the box. Wal, he finds the stateroom door all locked to be sure, and my lady had the key in her pocket; but then the cap'n he had a master key to it; and so he puts it in, and opens the door quite softly, and begins to take observations.

"Sure enough, he finds that the screws had been drawed from the top o' the box, showin' that the widder had been a tinkerin' on't when they thought she was a cryin' over it; and then, lookin' close, he sees a bit o' twine goin' from a crack in the box out o' the winder, and up on deck.

"Wal, the cap'n he kind o' got in the sperit o' the thing; and he thought he'd jest let the widder play her play out, and see what it would come to. So he jest calls Tom Toothacre down to him and whispered to him. 'Tom,' says he, 'you jest crawl under the berth in that 'are state-room, and watch that 'are box.' And Tom said he would.

"So Tom creeps under the berth, and lies there still as a mouse; and the cap'n he slips out and turns the key in the door, so that when madam comes down she shouldn't s'pect nothin'.

"Putty soon, sure enough, Tom heard the lock rattle, and the young widder come in; and then he heard a bit o' conversation between her and the corpse.

"'What time is it?' come in a kind o' hoarse whisper out o' the box.

"'Well, 'bout nine o'clock,' says she.

"'How long afore you'll let me out?' says he.

"'Oh I you must have patience,' says she, 'till they're all gone off to sleep; when there ain't but one man up. I can knock him down,' says she, 'and then I'll pull the string for you.'

"'The devil you will, ma'am!' says Tom to himself, under the berth.

"'Well, it's darned close here,' says the fellow in the box. He didn't say darned, boys; but he said a wickeder word that I can't repeat, noways," said Sam, in a parenthesis: "these 'ere British officers was drefful swearin' critters.

"'You must have patience a while longer,' says the lady, 'till I pull the string.' Tom Toothacre lay there on his back a laughin'.

"'Is every thing goin' on right?' says the man in the box.

"'All straight,' says she: 'there don't none of 'em suspect.'

"'You bet,' says Tom Toothacre, under the berth; and he said he had the greatest mind to catch the critter by the feet as she was a standin' there, but somehow thought it would be better fun to see the thing through 'cording as they'd planned it.

"Wal, then she went off switchin' and mincin' up to the deck agin, and a flirtin' with the cap'n; for you see 'twas 'greed to let 'em play their play out.

"Wal, Tom he lay there a waitin'; and he waited and waited and waited, till he 'most got asleep; but finally he heard a stirrin' in the box, as if the fellah was a gettin' up. Tom he jest crawled out still and kerful, and stood-up tight agin the wall. Putty soon he hears a grunt, and he sees the top o' the box a risin' up, and a man jest gettin' out on't mighty still.

"Wal, Tom he waited till he got fairly out on to the floor, and had his hand on the lock o' the door, when he jumps on him, and puts both arms round him, and gin him a regular bear's hug.

"'Why, what's this?' says the man.

"'Guess ye'll find out, darn ye,' says Tom Tooth-acre. 'So, ye wanted our ship, did ye? Wal, ye jest can't have our ship,' says Tom, says he; and I tell you he jest run that 'are fellow up stairs lickety-split, for Tom was strong as a giant.

"The fust thing they saw was Mr. More hed got the widder by both arms, and was tying on 'em behind her. 'Ye see, madam, your game's up,' says Mr. More, 'but we'll give ye a free passage to Boston, tho',' says he: 'we wanted a couple o' prisoners about these days, and you'll do nicely.'

"The fellers they was putty chopfallen, to be sure, and the one in women's clothes 'specially: 'cause when he was found out, he felt foolish enough in his petticuts; but they was both took to Boston, and given over as prisoners.

"Ye see, come to look into matters, they found these two young fellows, British officers, had formed a regular plot to take Cap'n Tucker's vessel, and run it into Halifax; and ye see, Cap'n Tucker he was so sort o' spry, and knew all the Maine coast so well, and was so 'cute at dodgin' in and out all them little bays and creeks and places all 'long shore, that he made the British considerable trouble, 'cause wherever they didn't want him, that's where he was sure to be.

"So they'd hatched up this 'ere plan. There was one or two British sailors had been and shipped aboard 'The Brilliant' a week or two aforehand, and 'twas suspected they was to have helped in the plot if thngs had gone as they laid out; but I tell you, when the fellows see which way the cat jumped, they took pretty good care to say that they hadn't nothin' to do with it. Oh, no, by no manner o' means! Wal, o' course, ye know, it couldn't be proved on 'em, and so we let it go.

"But I tell you, Cap'n Tucker he felt pretty cheap about his widder. The worst on't was, they do say Ma'am Tucker got hold of it; and you might know if a woman got hold of a thing like that she'd use it as handy as a cat would her claws. The women they can't no more help hittin' a fellow a clip and a rap when they've fairly got him, than a cat when she's ketched a mouse; and so I shouldn't wonder if the Commodore heard something about his widder every time he went home from his v'y-ages the longest day he had to live. I don't know nothin' 'bout it, ye know: I only kind o' jedge by what looks, as human natur' goes.

"But, Lordy massy! boys, 't wa'n't nothin' to be 'shamed of in the cap'n. Folks 'll have to answer for wus things at the last day than tryin' to do a kindness to a poor widder, now, I tell *you*. It's better to be took in doin' a good thing, than never try to do good; and it's my settled opinion," said Sam, taking up his mug of cider and caressing it tenderly, "it's my humble opinion, that the best sort o' folks is the easiest took in, 'specially by the women. I reely don't think I should a done a bit better myself."

Captain Kidd's Money

One of our most favorite legendary resorts was the old barn. Sam Lawson preferred it on many accounts. It was quiet and retired, that is to say, at such distance from his own house, that he could not hear if Hepsy called ever so loudly, and farther off than it would be convenient for that industrious and painstaking woman to follow him. Then there was the soft fragrant cushion of hay, on which his length of limb could be easily bestowed. Our barn had an upper loft with a swinging outer door that commanded a view of the old mill, the waterfall, and the distant windings of the river, with its grassy green banks, its graceful elm draperies, and its white flocks of water-lilies; and then on this Saturday afternoon we had Sam all to ourselves. It was a drowsy, dreamy October day, when the hens were lazily "craw, crawing," in a soft, conversational undertone with each other, as they scratched and picked the hay-seed under the barn windows. Below in the barn black Cæsar sat quietly hatchelling flax, sometimes gurgling and giggling to himself with an overflow of that interior jollity with which he seemed to be always full. The African in New England was a curious contrast to everybody around him in the joy and satisfaction that he seemed to feel in the mere fact of being alive. Every white person was glad or sorry for some appreciable cause in the past, present, or future, which was capable of being definitely stated; but black Cæsar was in an eternal giggle and frizzle and simmer of enjoyment for which he could give no earthly reason: he was an "embodied joy," like Shelley's skylark.

"Jest hear him," said Sam Lawson, looking pensively over the hay-mow, and strewing hayseed down on his wool. "How that 'are critter seems to tickle and laugh all the while 'bout nothin'. Lordy massy! he don't seem never to consider that 'this life's a dream, an empty show.'"

"Look here, Sam," we broke in, anxious to cut short a threatened stream of morality, "you promised to tell us about Capt. Kidd, and how you dug for his money."

"Did I, now? Wal, boys, that 'are history o' Kidd's is a warnin' to fellers. Why, Kidd had pious parents and Bible and sanctuary privileges when he was a boy, and yet come to be hanged. It's all in this 'ere song I'm a goin' to sing ye. Lordy massy! I wish I had my bass-viol now. – Cæsar," he said, calling down from his perch, "can't you strike the pitch o' 'Cap'n Kidd,' on your fiddle?"

Cæsar's fiddle was never far from him. It was, in fact, tucked away in a nice little nook just over the manger; and he often caught an interval from his work to scrape a dancing-tune on it, keeping time with his heels, to our great delight.

A most wailing minor-keyed tune was doled forth, which seemed quite refreshing to Sam's pathetic vein, as he sang in his most lugubrious tones, –

> "'My name was Robert Kidd
> As I sailed, as I sailed,
> My name was Robert Kidd;
> God's laws I did forbid,
> And so wickedly I did,
> As I sailed, as I sailed.'

"Now ye see, boys, he's a goin' to tell

how he abused his religious privileges;
just hear now: –

> "'My father taught me well,
> As I sailed, as I sailed;
> My father taught me well
> To shun the gates of hell,
> But yet I did rebel,
> As I sailed, as I sailed.

> "'He put a Bible in my hand,
> As I sailed, as I sailed;
> He put a Bible in my hand,
> And I sunk it in the sand
> Before I left the strand,
> As I sailed, as I sailed.'

"Did ye ever hear o' such a hardened,
contrary critter, boys? It's awful to think
on. Wal, ye see that 'are's the way
fellers allers begin the ways o' sin, by
turnin' their backs on the Bible and the
advice o' pious parents. Now hear what
he come to: –

> "'Then I murdered William More,
> As I sailed, as I sailed;
> I murdered William More,
> And left him in his gore,
> Not many leagues from shore,
> As I sailed, as I sailed.

"'To execution dock
I must go, I must go.
To execution dock,
While thousands round me flock,
To see me on the block,
I must go, I must go.'

"There was a good deal more on't," said Sam, pausing, "but I don't seem to remember it; but it's real solemn and affectin'."

"Who was Capt. Kidd, Sam?" said I.

"Wal, he was an officer in the British navy, and he got to bein' a pirate: used to take ships and sink 'em, and murder the folks; and so they say he got no end o' money, – gold and silver and precious stones, as many as the wise men in the East. But ye see, what good did it all do him? He couldn't use it, and dar'sn't keep it; so he used to bury it in spots round here and there in the awfullest heathen way ye ever heard of. Why, they say he allers used to kill one or two men or women or children of his prisoners, and bury with it, so that their sperits might keep watch on it ef anybody was to dig arter it. That 'are thing has been tried and tried and tried, but no man nor mother's son on 'em ever got a cent that dug. 'Twas tried here'n Oldtown; and they come pretty nigh gettin' on't, but it gin 'em the slip. Ye see, boys, *it's the Devil's money, and he holds a pretty tight grip on't.*"

"Well, how was it about digging for it? Tell us, did *you* do it? Were *you* there? Did you see it? And why couldn't they get it?" we both asked eagerly and in one breath.

"Why, Lordy massy! boys, your questions tumbles over each other thick as martins out o' a martin-box. Now, you jest be moderate and let alone, and I'll tell you all about it from the beginnin' to the end. I didn't railly have no hand in't, though I was know-in' to 't, as I be to most things that goes on round here; but my conscience wouldn't railly a let me start on no sich undertakin'.

"Wal, the one that fust sot the thing a goin' was old Mother Hokum, that used to live up in that little tumble-down shed by the cranberry-pond up beyond the spring pastur'. They had a putty bad name, them Hokums. How they got a livin' nobody knew; for they didn't seem to pay no attention to raisin' nothin' but childun, but the duce knows, there was plenty o' them. Their old hut was like a rabbit-pen: there was a tow-head to every crack and cranny. 'Member what old Cæsar said once when the word come to the store that old Hokum had got twins. 'S'pose de Lord knows best,' says Cæsar, 'but I thought dere was Hokums enough afore.' Wal, even poor workin' industrious folks like me finds it's hard gettin' along when there's so many mouths to feed. Lordy massy! there don't never seem to be no end on't, and so it ain't wonderful, come to think on't, ef folks like them Hokums gets tempted to help along in ways that ain't quite, right. Anyhow, folks did use to think that old Hokum was too sort o' familiar with their wood-piles 'long in the night, though they couldn't never prove it on him; and when Mother Hokum come to houses round to wash, folks use sometimes to miss pieces, here and there, though they never could find 'em on her; then they was allers a gettin' in debt here and a gottin' in debt there.

Why, they got to owin' two dollars to Joe Gidger for butcher's meat. Joe was sort o' good-natured and let 'em have meat, 'cause Hokum he promised so fair to pay; but he couldn't never get it out o' him. 'Member once Joe walked clear up to the cranberry-pond artor that 'are two dollars; but Mother Hokum she see him a comin' jest as he come past the juniper-bush on the corner. She says to Hokum, 'Get into bed, old man, quick, and let me tell the story,' says she. So she covered him up; and when Gidger come in she come up to him, and says she, 'Why, Mr. Gidger, I'm jest ashamed to see yo: why, Mr. Hokum was jest a comin' down to pay yo that 'are money last week, but ye see he was took down with the small-pox' – Joe didn't hear no mow: he just turned round, and he streaked it out that 'are door with his coat-tails flyin' out straight ahind him; and old Mother Hokum she jest stood at the window holdin' her sides and laughin' fit to split, to see him run. That 'are's jest a sample o' the ways them Hokums cut up.

"Wal, you see, boys, there's a queer kind o' rock down on the bank 'o the river, that looks sort o' like a grave-stone. The biggest part on't is sunk down under ground, and it's pretty well growed over with blackberry-vines; but, when you scratch the bushes away, they used to make out some queer marks on that 'are rock. They was sort o' lines and crosses; and folks would have it that them was Kidd's private marks, and that there was one o' the places where he hid his money.

"Wal, there's no sayin' fairly how it come to be thought so; but fellers used to say so, and they used sometimes to talk it over to the tahvern, and kind o' wonder whether or no, if they should dig, they wouldn't come to suthin'.

"Wal, old Mother Hokum she heard on't, and she was a sort o' enterprisin' old crittur: fact was, she had to be, 'cause the young Hokums was jest like bag-worms, the more they growed the more they eat, and I expect she found it pretty hard to fill their mouths; and so she said ef there *was* any thing under that 'are rock, they'd as good's have it as the Devil; and so she didn't give old Hokum no peace o' his life, but he must see what there was there.

"Wal, I was with 'em the night they was a talk-in' on't up. Ye see, Hokum he got thirty-seven cents' worth o' lemons and sperit. I see him goin' by as I was out a splittin' kindlin's; and says he, 'Sam, you jest go 'long up to our house to-night,' says he: 'Toddy Whitney and Harry Wiggin's com-in' up, and we're goin' to have a little suthin' hot,' says he; and he kind o' showed me the lemons and sperit. And I told him I guessed I would go 'long. Wal, I kind o' wanted to see what they'd be up to, ye know.

"Wal, come to find out, they was a talkin' about Cap'n Kidd's treasures, and layin' out how they should get it, and a settin' one another on with gret stories about it.

"'I've heard that there was whole chists full o' gold guineas,' says one.

"'And I've heard o' gold bracelets and ear-rings and finger-rings all sparklin' with diamonds,' says another.

"'Maybe it's old silver plate from some

117

o' them old West Indian grandees,' says another.

"'Wal, whatever it is,' says Mother Hokum, 'I want to be into it,' says she.

"'Wal, Sam, won't you jine?' says they.

"'Wal, boys,' says I, 'I kind o' don't feel jest like j'inin'. I sort o' ain't clear about the rights on't: seems to me it's mighty nigh like goin' to the Devil for money.'

"'Wal,' says Mother Hokum, 'what if 'tis? Money's money, get it how ye will; and the Devil's money 'll buy as much meat as any. I'd go to the Devil, if he gave good money.'

"'Wal, I guess I wouldn't,' says I. 'Don't you 'member the sermon Parson Lothrop preached about hastin' to be rich, last sabba' day?'

"'Parson Lothrop be hanged!' says she. 'Wal, now,' says she, 'I like to see a parson with his silk stockin's and great gold-headed cane, a lollopin' on his carriage behind his fat, prancin' hosses, comin' to meetin' to preach to us poor folks not to want to be rich! How'd he like it to have forty-'leven children, and nothin' to put onto 'em or into 'em, I wonder? Guess if Lady Lothrop had to rub and scrub, and wear her fingers to the bone as I do, she'd want to be rich; and I guess the parson, if he couldn't get a bellyful for a week, would be for diggin' up Kidd's money, or doing 'most any thing else to make the pot bile.'

"'Wal,' says I, 'I'll kind o' go with ye, boys, and sort o' see how things turn out; but I guess I won't take no shere in't,' says I.

"Wal, they got it all planned out. They was to wait till the full moon, and then they was to get Primus King to go with 'em and help do the diggin'. Ye see, Hokum and Toddy Whitney and Wiggin are all putty softly fellers, and hate dreffully to work; and I tell you the Kidd money ain't to be got without a pretty tough piece o' diggin. Why, it's jest like diggin' a well to get at it. Now, Primus King was the master hand for diggin' wells, and so they said they'd get him by givin' on him a shere.

"Harry Wiggin he didn't want no nigger a

sherin' in it, he said; but Toddy and Hokum they said that when there was such stiff diggin' to be done, they didn't care if they did go in with a nigger.

"Wal, Wiggin he said he hadn't no objection to havin' the nigger do the diggin,' it was *sherin' the profits* he objected to.

"'Wal,' says Hokum, 'you can't get him without,' says he. 'Primus knows too much,' says he: 'you can't fool him.' Finally they 'greed that they was to give Primus twenty dollars, and shere the treasure 'mong themselves.

"Come to talk with Primus, he wouldn't stick in a spade, unless they'd pay him aforehand. Ye see, Primus was up to 'em; he knowed about Gidger, and there wa'n't none on 'em that was particular good pay; and so they all jest hed to rake and scrape, and pay him down the twenty dollars among 'em; and they 'greed for the fust full moon, at twelve' o'clock at night, the 9th of October.

"Wal, ye see I had to tell Hepsy I was goin' out to watch. Wal, so I was; but not jest in the way she took it: but, Lordy massy! a feller has to tell his wife suthin' to keep her quiet, ye know, 'specially Hepsy.

"Wal, wal, of all the moonlight nights that ever I did see, I never did see one equal to that. Why, you could see the color o' every thing. I 'member I could see how the huckleberry-bushes on the rock was red as blood when the moonlight shone through 'em; 'cause the leaves, you see, had begun to turn.

"Goin' on our way we got to talkin' about the sperits.

"'I ain't afraid on 'em,' says Hokum. 'What harm can a sperit do me?' says he. 'I don't care ef there's a dozen on 'em;' and he took a swig at his bottle.

"'Oh! there ain't no sperits,' says Harry Wiggin. 'That 'are talk's all nonsense;' and he took a swig at *his* bottle.

"'Wal,' says Toddy, 'I don't know 'bout that 'are. Me and Ike Sanders has seen the sperits in the Cap'n Brown house. We thought we'd jest have a peek into the window one night; and there was a whole flock o' black colts without no heads on come rushin' on us and knocked us flat.'

"'I expect you'd been at the tahvern,' said Hokum.

"'Wal, yes, we had; but them was sperits: we wa'n't drunk, now; we was jest as sober as ever we was.'

"'Wal, they won't get away my money,' says Primus, for I put it safe away in Dinah's teapot afore I come out;' and then he showed all his ivories from ear to ear. 'I think all this 'are's sort o' foolishness,' says Primus.

"'Wal,' says I, 'boys, I ain't a goin' to have no part or lot in this 'ere matter, but I'll jest lay it off to you how it's to be done. Ef Kidd's money is under this rock, there's 'sperits' that watch it, and you mustn't give 'em no advantage. There mustn't be a word spoke from the time ye get sight o' the treasure till ye get it safe up on to firm ground,' says I. 'Ef ye do, it'll vanish right out o' sight. I've talked with them that has dug down to it and seen it; but they allers lost it, 'cause they'd call out and say suthin'; and the minute they spoke, away it went.'

"Wal, so they marked off the ground; and Primus he begun to dig, and the rest kind o' sot round. It was so still it was kind o' solemn. Ye see, it was past twelve o'clock, and every critter in Oldtown was asleep; and there was two whippoorwills on the great Cap'n Brown elm-trees, that kep' a answerin' each other back and forward sort o' solitary like; and then every once in a while there'd come a sort o' strange whisper up among the elm-tree leaves, jest as if there was talkin' goin' on; and every time Primus struck his spade into the ground it sounded sort o' holler, jest as if he'd been a diggin' a grave. 'It's kind o' melancholy,' says I, 'to think o' them poor critters that had to be killed and buried jest to keep this 'ere treasure. What awful things 'll be brought to light in the judgment day! Them poor critters they loved to live and hated to die as much as any on us; but no, they hed to die jest to satisfy that critter's wicked will. I've heard them as thought they could tell the Cap'n Kidd places by layin' their ear to the ground at midnight, and they'd hear groans and wailin's."

"Why, Sam! were there really people who could tell where Kidd's money was?" I here interposed.

"Oh, sartin! why, yis. There was Shebna Basconx, he was one. Shebna could always tell what was under the earth. He'd cut a hazel-stick, and hold it in his hand when folks was wantin' to know where to dig wells; and that 'are stick would jest turn in his hand, and p'int down till it would fairly grind the bark off; and ef you dug in that place you was sure to find a spring. Oh, yis! Shebna he's told many where the Kidd money was, and been with 'em when they dug for it; but the pester on't was they allers lost it, 'cause they would some on 'em speak afore they thought."

"But, Sam, what about this digging? Let's know what came of it," said we, as Sam appeared to lose his way in his story.

"Wal, ye see, they dug down about five feet, when Primus he struck his spade smack on something that chincked like iron.

"Wal, then Hokum and Toddy Whitney

was into the hole in a minute: they made Primus get out, and they took the spade, 'cause they wanted to be sure to come on it themselves.

"Wal, they begun, and they dug and he scraped, and sure enough they come to a gret iron pot as big as your granny's dinner-pot, with an iron bale to it.

"Wal, then they put down a rope, and he put the rope through the handle; then Hokum and Toddy they clambered upon the bank, and all on 'em began to draw, up jest as still and silent as could be. They drawed and they drawed, till they jest got it even with the ground, when Toddy spoke out all in a tremble, 'There,'. says he, *'we've got it!'* And the minit he spoke they was both struck by *suthin* that knocked 'em clean over; and the rope give a crack like a pistol-shot, and broke short off; and the pot went down, down, down, and they heard it goin', jink, jink, jink; and it went way down into the earth, and the ground closed over it; and then they heard the screechin'est laugh ye ever did hear."

"I want to know, Sam, did you see that

pot?" I exclaimed at this part of the story.

"Wal, no, I didn't. Ye see, I jest happened to drop asleep while they was diggin', I was so kind o' tired, and I didn't wake up till it was all over.

"I was waked up, 'cause there was consid'able of a scuffle; for Hokum was so mad at Toddy for speakin', that he was a fistin' on him; and old Primus he jest haw-hawed and laughed. 'Wal, I got *my* money safe, anyhow,' says he.

"'Wal, come to,' says I. ''Tain't no use cryin' for spilt milk: you've jest got to turn in now and fill up this 'ere hole, else the selectmen 'll be down on ye.'

"'Wal,' says Primus, 'I didn't engage to fill up no holes;' and he put his spade on his shoulder and trudged off.

"Wal, it was putty hard work, fillin' in that hole; but Hokum and Toddy and Wiggin had to do it, 'cause they didn't want to have everybody a laughin' at 'em; and I kind o' tried to set it home to 'em, showin' on 'em that 'twas all for the best.

"'Ef you'd a been left to get that 'are money, there'd a come a cuss with it,' says I. 'It shows the vanity o' hastin' to be rich.'

"'Oh, you shet up!' says Hokum, says he. 'You never hasted to any thing,' says he. Ye see, he was riled, that's why he spoke so."

"Sam," said we, after maturely reflecting over the story, "what do you suppose was in that pot?"

"Lordy massy! boys: ye never will be done askin' questions. Why, how should I know?"

"Mis' Elderkin's Pitcher."

"Ye see, boys," said Sam Lawson, as we were gathering young wintergreen on a sunny hillside in June, —"ye see, folks don't allers know what their marcies is when they sees 'em. Folks is kind o' blinded; and, when a providence comes along, they don't seem to know how to take it, and they growl and grumble about what turns out the best things that ever happened to 'em in their lives. It's like Mis' Elderkin's pitcher."

"What about Mis' Elderkin's pitcher?" said both of us in one breath.

"Didn't I never tell ye, now?" said Sam: "why, I wanter know?"

No, we were sure he never had told us; and Sam, as usual, began clearing the ground by a thorough introduction, with statistical expositions.

"Wal, ye see, Mis' Elderkin she lives now over to Sherburne in about the handsomest house in Sherburne, – a high white house, with green blinds and white pillars in front, – and she rides out in her own kerridge; and Mr. Elderkin, he 's a deakin in the church, and a colonel in the malitia, and a s'lectman, and pretty much atop every thing there is goin' in Sherburne, and it all come of that 'are pitcher."

"What pitcher?" we shouted in chorus.

"Lordy massy! that 'are 's jest what I'm a goin' to tell you about; but, ye see, a feller's jest got to make a beginnin' to all things.

"Mis' Elderkin she thinks she's a gret lady nowadays, I s'pose; but I 'member when she was Miry Brown over here 'n Oldtown, and I used to be waitin' on her to singing-school.

"Miry and I was putty good friends along in them days, – we was putty consid'able kind o' intimate. Fact is, boys, there was times in them days when I thought whether or no I wouldn't *take* Miry myself," said Sam, his face growing luminous with the pleasing idea of his former masculine attractions and privileges. "Yis," he continued, "there was a time when folks said I could a hed Miry ef I'd asked her; and I putty much think so myself, but I didn't say nothin': marriage is allers kind o'ventursome; an' Miry had such up-and-down kind o' ways, I was sort o' fraid on't.

"But Lordy massy! boys, you mustn't never tell Hepsy I said so, 'cause she'd be mad enough to bite a shingle-nail in two. Not that she sets so very gret by me neither; but then women's backs is allers up ef they think anybody else could a hed you, whether they want you themselves or not.

"Ye see, Miry she was old Black Hoss John Brown's da'ter, and lived up there in that 'are big brown house by the meetin'-house, that hes the red hollyhock in the front yard. Miry was about the handsomest gal that went into the singers' seat a Sunday.

"I tell you she wa'n't none o' your milk-and-sugar gals neither, – she was 'mazin' strong built. She was the strongest gal in her arms that I ever see. Why, I 've seen Miry take up a barrel o' flour, and lift it right into the kitchen; and it would jest make the pink come into her cheeks like two roses, but she never seemed to mind it a grain. She had a good strong back of her own, and she was straight as a poplar, with snappin' black eyes, and I tell you there was a snap to her tongue too. Nobody never got ahead o' Miry; she'd give every fellow as good as he sent, but for all that she was a gret favorite.

"Miry was one o' your briery, scratchy gals, that seems to catch fellers in thorns. She allers fit and flouted her beaux, and the more she fit and flouted 'em the more they 'd be arter her. There wa'n't a gal in all Oldtown that led such a string o' fellers arter her; 'cause, you see, she'd now and then throw 'em a good word over her shoulder, and then they 'd all fight who should get it, and she'd jest laugh to see 'em do it.

"Why, there was Tom Sawin, he was one o' her beaux, and Jim Moss, and Ike Bacon; and there was a Boston boy, Tom Beacon, he came up from Cambridge to rusticate with Parson Lothrop; he thought he must have his say with Miry, but he got pretty well come up with. You see, he thought 'cause he was Boston born that he was kind o' aristocracy, and hed a right jest to pick and choose 'mong country gals; but the way he got come up with by Miry was too funny for any thing."

"Do tell us about it," we said, as Sam made an artful pause, designed to draw forth solicitation.

"Wal, ye see, Tom Beacon he told Ike Bacon about it, and Ike he told me. 'Twas this way. Ye see, there was a quiltin' up to Mis' Cap'n Broad's, and Tom Beacon he was there; and come to goin' home with the gals, Tom he cut Ike out, and got Miry all to himself; and 'twas a putty long piece of a walk from Mis' Cap'n Broad's up past the swamp and the stone pastur' clear up to old Black Hoss John's.

"Wal, Tom he was in high feather 'cause Miry took him, so that he didn't reelly know how to behave; and so, as they was walkin' along past Parson Lothrop's apple-orchard, Tom thought he'd try bein' familiar, and he undertook to put his arm round Miry. Wal, if she didn't jest take that little fellow by his two shoulders and whirl him over the fence into the orchard quicker 'n no time. 'Why,' says Tom, 'the fust I knew I was lyin' on my back under the apple-trees lookin' up at the stars.' Miry she jest walked off home and said nothin' to nobody, – it wa'n't her way to talk much about things; and, if it hedn't ben for Tom Beacon himself, nobody need 'a' known nothin' about it. Tom was a little fellow, you see, and 'mazin' good-natured, and one o' the sort that couldn't keep nothin' to himself; and so he let the cat out o' the bag himself. Wal, there didn't nobody think the worse o' Miry. When fellers find a gal won't take saace from no man, they kind o' respect her; and then fellers allers thinks ef it hed ben *them*, now, things 'd 'a' been different. That's jest what Jim Moss and Ike Bacon said: they said, why Tom Beacon was a fool not to know better how to get along with Miry, – *they* never had no trouble. The fun of it was, that Tom Beacon himself was more crazy after her than he was afore; and they say he made Miry a right up-and-down offer, and Miry she jest wouldn't have him.

"Wal, you see, that went agin old Black

Hoss John's idees: old Black Hoss was about as close as a nut and as contrairy as a pipperage-tree. You ought to 'a' seen him. Why, his face was all a perfect crisscross o' wrinkles. There wa'n't a spot where you could put a pin down that there wa'n't a wrinkle; and they used to say that he held on to every cent that went through his fingers till he'd pinched it into two. You couldn't say that his god was his belly, for he hedn't none, no more'n an old file: folks said that he'd starved himself till the moon'd shine through him.

"Old Black Hoss was awfully grouty about Miry's refusin' Tom Beacon, 'cause there was his houses and lots o' land in Boston. A drefful worldly old critter Black Hoss John was: he was like the rich fool in the gospel. Wal, he's dead and gone now, poor critter, and what good has it all done him? It's as the Scriptur' says, 'He heapeth up riches, and knoweth not who shall gather them.'

"Miry hed a pretty hard row to hoe with old Black Hoss John. She was up early and down late, and kep' every thing a goin'. She made the cheese and made the butter, and between spells she braided herself handsome straw bunnets, and fixed up her clothes; and somehow she worked it so when she sold her butter and cheese that there was somethin' for ribbins and flowers. You know the Scriptur' says, 'Can a maid forget her ornaments?' Wal, Miry didn't. I 'member I used to lead the singin' in them days, and Miry she used to sing counter, so we sot putty near together in the singers' seats; and I used to think Sunday mornin's when she come to meetin' in her white dress and her red cheeks, and her bunnet all tipped off with laylock, that 'twas for all the world jest like sunshine to have her come into the singers' seats. Them was the days that I didn't improve my privileges, boys," said Sam, sighing deeply. "There was times that ef I'd a spoke, there's no knowin' what mightn't 'a' happened, 'cause, you see, boys, I was better lookin' in them days than I be now. Now you mind, boys, when you grow up, ef you get to waitin' on a nice gal, and you're 'most a mind to speak up to her, don't you go and put it off, 'cause, ef you do, you may live to repent it.

"Wal, you see, from the time that Bill Elderkin come and took the academy, I could see plain enough that it was time for me to hang up my fiddle. Bill he used to set in the singers' seats, too, and he would have it that he sung tenor. He no more sung tenor than a skunk-blackbird; but he made b'lieve he did, jest to git next to Miry in the singers' seats. They used to set there in the seats a writin' backward and forward to each other till they tore out all the leaves of the hymn-books, and the singin'-books besides. Wal, I never thought that the house o' the Lord was jest the place to be courtin' in, and I used to get consid'able shocked at the way things went on atween 'em. Why, they'd be a writin' all sermon-time; and I've seen him a lookin' at her all through the long prayer in a way that wa'n't right, considerin' they was both professors of religion. But then the fact was, old Black Hoss John was to blame for it, 'cause he never let 'em have no chance to hum. Ye see, old Black Hoss he was sot agin Elderkin 'cause he was poor. You see, his mother, the old Widdah Elderkin, she was jest about the poorest, peakedest old body over to

Sherburne, and went out to days' works; and Bill Elderkin he was all for books and larnin', and old Black Hoss John he thought it was just shiftlessness: but Miry she thought he was a genius; and she got it sot in her mind that he was goin' to be President o' the United States, or some sich.

"Wal, old Black Hoss he wa'n't none too polite to Miry's beaux in gineral, but when Elderkin used to come to see her he was snarlier than a saw: he hadn't a good word for him noways; and he'd rake up the fire right before his face and eyes, and rattle about fastenin' up the windows, and tramp up to bed, and call down the chamber-stairs to Miry to go to bed, and was sort o' aggravatin' every way.

"Wal, ef folks wants to get a gal set on havin' a man, that 'ere's the way to go to work. Miry had a consid'able stiff will of her own; and, ef she didn't care about Tom Beacon before, she hated him now; and, if she liked Bill Elderkin before, she was clean gone over to him now. And so she took to goin' to the Wednesday-evenin' lecture, and the Friday-even-in' prayer-meetin', and the singin'-school, jest as regular as a clock, and so did he; and arterwards they allers walked home the longest way. Fathers may jest as well let their gals be courted in the house, peaceable, 'cause, if they can't be courted there, they'll find places where they can be: it's jest human natur'.

"Wal, come fall, Elderkin he went to college up to Brunswick; and then I used to see the letters as regular up to the store every week, comin' in from Brunswick, and old Black Hoss John he see 'em too, and got a way of droppin' on 'em in his coat-pocket when he come up to the store, and folks used to say that the letters that went into his coat-pocket didn't get to Miry. Anyhow, Miry she says to me one day says she, 'Sam, you're up round the post-office a good deal,' says she. 'I wish, if you see any letters for me, you'd jest bring 'em along.' I see right into it, and I told her to be sure I would; and so I used to have the carryin' of great thick letters every week. Wal, I was waitin' on Hepsy along about them times, and so Miry and I kind o' sympathized. Hepsy was a pretty gal, and I thought it was all best as 'twas;

any way, I knew I couldn't get Miry, and I could get Hepsy, and that made all the difference in the world.

"Wal, that next winter old Black Hoss was took down with rheumatism, and I tell you if Miry didn't have a time on't! He wa'n't noways sweet-tempered when he was well; but come to be crooked up with the rheumatis' and kep' awake nights, it seemed as if he was determined there shouldn't nobody have no peace so long as he couldn't.

"He'd get Miry up and down with him night after night a makin' her heat flannels and vinegar, and then he'd jaw and scold so that she was eenymost beat out. He wouldn't have nobody set up with him, though there was offers made. No: he said Miry was his daughter, and 'twas her bisness to take care on him.

"Miry was clear worked down: folks kind o' pitied her. She was a strong gal, but there's things that wears out the strongest. The worst on't was, it hung on so. Old Black Hoss had a most amazin' sight o' constitution. He'd go all down to death's door, and seem hardly to have the breath, o' life in him, and then up he'd come agin! These 'ere old folks that nobody wants to have live allers hev such a sight o' wear in 'em, they jest last and last; and it really did seem as if he'd wear Miry out and get her into the grave fust, for she got a cough with bein' up so much in the cold, and grew thin as a shadder. 'Member one time I went up there to offer to watch jest in the spring o' the year, when the laylocks was jest a buddin' out, and Miry she come and talked with me over the fence; and the poor gal she fairly broke down, and sobbed as if her heart would break, a tellin' me her trouble.

"Wal, it reelly affected me more to have Miry give up so than most gals, 'cause she'd allers held her head up, and hed sich a sight o' grit and resolution; but she told me all about it.

"It seems old Black Hoss he wa'n't content with worryin' on her, and gettin' on her up nights, but he kep' a hectorin' her about Bill Elderkin, and wantin' on her to promise that she wouldn't hev Bill when he was dead and gone; and Miry she wouldn't promise, and then the old man said she shouldn't have a cent from him if she didn't, and so they had it back and forth. Everybody in town was sayin' what a shame 'twas that he should sarve her so; for though he hed other children, they was married and gone, and there wa'n't none of them to do for him but jest Miry.

"Wal, he hung on till jest as the pinys in the front yard was beginnin' to blow out, and then he began, to feel he was a goin', and he sent for Parson Lothrop to know what was to be done about his soul.

"'Wal,' says Parson Lothrop, 'you must settle up all your worldly affairs; you must be in peace and love with all mankind; and, if you've wronged anybody, you must make it good to 'em.'

"Old Black Hoss he bounced right over in his bed with his back to the minister.

"'The devil!' says he: ''twill take all I've got.' And he never spoke another word, though Parson Lothrop he prayed with him, and did what he could for him.

"Wal, that night I sot up with him; and he went off 'tween two and three in the mornin', and I laid him out regular. Of all the racks o' bone I ever see, I never see a human critter so poor as he was. 'Twa'n't nothin' but his awful will kep' his soul in his body so long, as it was.

"We had the funeral in the meetin'-house a Sunday; and Parson Lothrop he preached a sarmon on contentment on the text, 'We brought nothin' into the world, and it's sartin we can carry nothin' out; and having food and raiment, let us be therewith content.' Parson Lothrop he got round the subject about as handsome as he could: he didn't say what a skinflint old Black Hoss was, but he talked in a gineral way about the vanity o' worryin' an' scrapin' to heap up riches. Ye see, Parson Lothrop he could say it all putty easy, too, 'cause since he married a rich wife he never hed no occasion to worry about temporal matters. Folks allers preaches better on the vanity o' riches when they's in tol'able easy circumstances. Ye see, when folks is pestered and worried to pay their bills, and don't know where the next dollar's to come from, it's a great temptation to be kind o' valooin' riches, and mebbe envyin' those that's got 'em; whereas when one's accounts all pays themselves, and the money comes jest when its wanted regular, a body feels sort o' composed like, and able to take the right view o' things, like Parson Lothrop.

"Wal, arter sermon the relations all went over to the old house to hear the will read; and, as I was kind o' friend with the family, I jest slipped in along with the rest.

"Squire Jones he had the will; and so when they all got sot round all solemn, he broke the seals and unfolded it, cracklin' it a good while afore he begun; and it was so still you might a heard a pin drop when he begun to read. Fust, there was the farm and stock, he left to his son John Brown over in Sherburne. Then there was the household stuff and all them things, spoons and dishes, and beds and kiver-lids, and so on, to his da'ter Polly Blanchard. And then, last of all, he says, he left to his da'ter Miry *the pitcher that was on the top o' the shelf in his bedroom closet.*

"That 'are was an old cracked pitcher that Miry allers hed hated the sight of, and spring and fall she used to beg her father to let her throw it away; but no, he wouldn't let her touch it, and so it stood gatherin' dust.

"Some on 'em run and handed it down; and it seemed jest full o' scourin'-sand and nothin' else, and they handed it to Miry.

"Wal, Miry she was wrathy then. She didn't so much mind bein' left out in the will, 'cause she expected that; but to have that 'are old pitcher poked at her so sort o' scornful was more'n she could bear.

"She took it and gin it a throw across the room with all her might; and it hit agin the wall and broke into a thousand bits, when out rolled hundreds of gold pieces; great gold eagles and guineas flew round the kitchen jest as thick as dandelions in a meadow. I tell you, she scrabbled them up pretty quick, and we all helped her.

"Come to count 'em over, Miry had the best fortin of the whole, as 'twas right and proper she should. Miry she was a sensible gal, and she invested her money well; and so, when Bill Elderkin got through his law-studies, he found a wife that could make a nice beginnin' with him. And that's the way, you see, they came to be doin' as well as they be.

"So, boys, you jest mind and remember and allers see what there is in a providence afore you quarrel with it, 'cause there's a good many things in this world turns out like Mis' Elderkin's pitcher."

The Ghost in the Cap'n Brownhouse

"Now, Sam, tell us certain true, is there any such things as ghosts?"

"Be there ghosts?" said Sam, immediately translating into his vernacular grammar: "wal, now, that are's jest the question, ye see." "Well, grandma thinks there are, and Aunt Lois thinks it's all nonsense. Why, Aunt Lois don't even believe the stories in Cotton Mather's 'Magnalia.'"

"Wanter know?" said Sam, with a tone of slow, languid meditation.

We were sitting on a bank of the Charles River, fishing. The soft melancholy red of evening was fading off in streaks on the glassy water, and the houses of Oldtown were beginning to loom through the gloom, solemn and ghostly. There are times and tones and moods of nature that make all the vulgar, daily real seem shadowy, vague, and supernatural, as if the outlines of this hard material present were fading into the invisible and unknown. So Oldtown, with its elm-trees, its great square white houses, its meeting-house and tavern and blacksmith's shop and milly which at high noon seem as real and as commonplace as possible, at this hour of the evening were dreamy and solemn. They rose up blurred, indistinct, dark; here and there winking candles sent long lines of light through the shadows, and little drops of unforeseen rain rippled the sheeny darkness of the water.

"Wal, you see, boys, in them things it's jest as well to mind your granny. There's a consid'able sight o' gumption in grandmas. You look at the folks that's alius tellin' you what they don't believe, – they don't believe this, and they don't believe that, – and what sort o' folks is they? Why, like yer Aunt Lois, sort o' stringy and dry. There ain't no 'sorption got out o' not believin' nothin'.

"Lord a massy! we don't know nothin' 'bout them things. We hain't ben there, and can't say that there ain't no ghosts and sich; can we, now?"

We agreed to that fact, and sat a little closer to Sam in the gathering gloom.

"Tell us about the Cap'n Brown house, Sam."

"Ye didn't never go over the Cap'n Brown house?"

No, we had not that advantage.

"Wal, yer see, Cap'n Brown he made all his money to sea, in furrin parts, and then come here to Oldtown to settle down.

"Now, there ain't no knowin' 'bout these 'ere old ship-masters, where they's ben, or what they's ben a doin', or how they got their money. Ask me no questions, and I'll tell ye no lies, is 'bout the best philosophy for them. Wal, it didn't do no good to ask Cap'n Brown questions too close, 'cause you didn't git no satisfaction. Nobody rightly knew 'bout who his folks was, or where they come from; and, ef a body asked him, he used to say that the very fust he know'd 'bout himself he was a young man walkin' the streets in London.

"But, yer see, boys, he hed money, and that is about all folks wanter know when a man comes to settle down. And he bought that 'are place, and built that 'are house. He built it all sea-cap'n fashion, so's to feel as much at home as he could. The parlor was like a ship's cabin. The table and chairs was fastened down to the floor, and the closets was made with holes to set the casters and the decanters and bottles in, jest's they be at sea; and there was stanchions to hold on by; and they say that blowy nights the cap'n used to fire up pretty well with his grog, till he hed about all he could carry, and then he'd set and hold on, and hear the wind blow, and kind o' feel out to sea right there to hum. There wasn't no Mis' Cap'n Brown, and there didn't seem likely to be none. And whether there ever hed been one, nobody know'd. He hed an old black Guinea nigger-woman, named Quassia, that did his work. She was shaped pretty much like one o' these 'ere great crookneck-squashes. She wa'n't no gret beauty, I can tell you; and she used to wear a gret red turban and a yaller short gown and red petticoat, and a gret string o' gold beads round her neck, and gret big gold hoops in her ears, made right in the middle o' Africa among the heathen there. For all she was black, she thought a heap o' herself, and was consid'able sort o' predominative over the cap'n. Lordy massy! boys, it's alius so. Get a man and a woman together, – any sort o' woman you're a mind to, don't care who 'tis, – and one way or another she gets the rule over him, and he jest has to train to her fife. Some does it one way, and some does it another; some does it by jawin' and some does it by kissin', and some does it by faculty and contrivance; but one way or another they allers does it. Old Cap'n Brown was a good stout, stocky kind o' John Bull sort o' fellow, and a good judge o' sperits, and allers kep' the best in them are cupboards o' his'n; but, fust and last, things in his house went pretty much as old Quassia said.

"Folks got to kind o' respectin' Quassia. She come to meetin' Sunday regular, and sot all fixed up in red and yaller and green, with glass beads and what not, lookin' for all the world like one o' them ugly Indian idols; but she was well-behaved as any Christian. She was a master hand at cookin'. Her bread and biscuits couldn't be beat, and no couldn't her pies, and there wa'n't no such pound-cake as she made nowhere. Wal, this 'ere story I'm a goin' to tell you was told me by Cinthy Pendleton. There ain't a more respectable gal, old or young, than Cinthy nowheres. She lives over to Sherburne now, and I hear tell she's sot up a manty-makin' business; but then she used to do tailorin' in Oldtown. She was a member o' the church, and a good Christian as ever was. Wal, ye see, Quassia she got Cinthy to come up and spend a week to the Cap'n Brown house, a doin' tailorin' and a fixin' over his close: 'twas along toward the fust o' March. Cinthy she sot by the fire in the front parlor with her goose and her press-board and her work: for there wa'n't no company callin', and the snow was drifted four feet deep right across the front door;

so there wa'n't much danger o' any body comin' in. And the cap'n he was a perlite man to wimmen; and Cinthy she liked it jest as well not to have company, 'cause the cap'n he'd make himself entertainin' tellin' on her sea-stories, and all about his adventures among the Ammonites, and Perresites, and Jebusites, and all sorts o' heathen people he'd been among.

"Wal, that 'are week there come on the master snow-storm. Of all the snow-storms that hed ben, that 'are was the beater; and I tell you the wind blew as if 'twas the last chance it was ever goin' to hev. Wal, it's kind o' scary like to be shet up in a lone house with all natur' a kind o' breakin' out, and goin' on so, and the snow a comin' down so thick ye can't see 'cross the street, and the wind a pipin' and a squeelin' and a rumblin' and a tumblin' fust down this chimney and then down that. I tell you, it sort o' sets a feller thinkin' o' the three great things, – death, judgment, and etarnaty; and I don't care who the folks is, nor how good they be, there's times when they must be feelin' putty consid'able solemn.

"Wal, Cinthy she said she kind o' felt so along, and she hed a sort o' queer feelin' come over her as if there was somebody or somethin' round the house more'n appeared. She said she sort o' felt it in the air; but it seemed to her silly, and she tried to get over it. But two or three times, she said, when it got to be dusk, she felt somebody go by her up the stairs. The front entry wa'n't very light in the daytime, and in the storm, come five o'clock, it was so dark that all you could see was jest a gleam o' some-thin', and two or three times when she started to go up stairs she see a soft white suthin' that seemed goin' up before her, and she stopped with her heart a beatin' like a trip-hammer, and she sort o' saw it go up and along the entry to the cap'n's door, and then it seemed to go right through, 'cause the door didn't open.

"Wal, Cinthy says she to old Quassia, says she, 'Is there anybody lives in this house but us?'

"'Anybody lives here?' says Quassia: 'what you mean?' says she.

"Says Cinthy, 'I thought somebody went past me on the stairs last night and to-night.'

"Lordy massy! how old Quassia did screech and laugh. 'Good Lord!' says she, 'how foolish white folks is! Somebody went past you? Was't the capt'in?'

"'No, it wa'n't the cap'n,' says she: 'it was somethin' soft and white, and moved very still; it was like somethin' in the air,' says she. Then Quassia she haw-hawed louder. Says she, 'It's hysterikes, Miss Cinthy; that's all it is.'

"Wal, Cinthy she was kind o' 'shamed, but for all that she couldn't help herself. Sometimes evenin's she'd be a settin' with the cap'n, and she'd think she'd hear somebody a movin' in his room overhead; and she knowed it wa'n't Quassia, 'cause Quassia was ironin' in the kitchen. She took pains once or twice to find out that 'are.

"Wal, ye see, the cap'n's room was the gret front upper chamber over the parlor, and then right oppi-site to it was the gret spare chamber where

Cinthy slept. It was jest as grand as could be, with a gret four-post mahogany bedstead and damask curtains brought over from England; but it was cold enough to freeze a white bear solid, – the way spare chambers allers is. Then there was the entry between, run straight through the house: one side was old Quassia's room, and the other was a sort o' storeroom, where the old cap'n kep' all sorts o' traps.

"Wal, Cinthy she kep' a hevin' things happen and a seein' things, till she didn't railly know what was in it. Once when she come into the parlor jest at sundown, she was sure she see a white figure a vanishin' out o' the door that went towards the side entry. She said it was so dusk, that all she could see was jest this white figure, and it jest went out still as a cat as she come in.

"Wal, Cinthy didn't like to speak to the cap'n about it. She was a close woman, putty prudent, Cinthy was.

"But one night, 'bout the middle o' the week, this 'ere thing kind o' come to a crisis.

"Cinthy said she'd ben up putty late a sewin' and a finishin' off down in the parlor; and the cap'n he sot up with her, and was consid'able cheerful and entertainin', tellin' her all about things over in the Bermudys, and off to Chiny and Japan, and round the world ginerally. The storm that hed been a blowin' all the week was about as furious as ever; and the cap'n he stirred up a mess o' flip, and hed it for her hot to go to bed on. He was a good-natured critter, and allers had feelin's for lone women; and I s'pose he knew 'twas sort o' desolate for Cinthy.

"Wal, takin' the flip so right the last thing afore goin' to bed, she went right off to sleep as sound as a nut, and slep' on till somewhere about mornin', when she said somethin' waked her broad awake in a minute. Her eyes flew wide open like a spring, and the storm hed gone down and the moon come out; and there, standin' right in the moonlight by her bed, was a woman jest as white as a sheet, with black hair hangin' down to her waist, and the brightest, mourn fullest black eyes you ever see. She stood there lookin' right at Cinthy; and Cinthy thinks that was what waked her up; 'cause, you know, ef anybody stands and looks steady at folks asleep it's apt to wake 'em.

"Any way, Cinthy said she felt jest as ef she was turnin' to stone. She couldn't move nor speak. She lay a minute, and then she shut her eyes, and begun to say her prayers; and a minute after she opened 'em, and it was gone.

"Cinthy was a sensible gal, and one that allers hed her thoughts about her; and she jest got up and put a shawl round her shoulders, and went first and looked at the doors, and they was both on 'em locked jest as she left 'em when she went to bed. Then she looked under the bed and in the closet, and felt all round the room: where she couldn't see she felt her way, and there wa'n't nothin' there.

"Wal, next mornin' Cinthy got up and went home, and she kep' it to herself a good while. Finally, one day when she was workin' to our house she told Hepsy about it, and Hepsy she told me."

"Well, Sam," we said, after a pause, in which we heard only the rustle of leaves and the ticking of branches against each other, "what do you suppose it was?"

"Wal, there 'tis: you know jest as much about it as I do. Hepsy told Cinthy it might 'a' ben a dream; so it might, but Cinthy she was sure it wa'n't a dream, 'cause she remembers plain hearin' the old clock on the stairs strike four while she had her eyes open lookin' at the woman; and then she only shet 'em a minute, jest to say 'Now I lay me,' and opened 'em and she was gone.

"Wal, Cinthy told Hepsy, and Hepsy she kep' it putty close. She didn't tell it to nobody except Aunt Sally Dickerson and the Widder Bije Smith and your Grandma Badger and the minister's wife; and they every one o' 'em 'greed it ought to be kep' close, 'cause it would make talk. Wal, come spring, somehow or other it seemed to 'a' got all over Old-town. I heard on 't to the store and up to the tavern; and Jake Marshall he says to me one day, 'What's this 'ere about the cap'n's house?' And the Widder Loker she says to me, 'There's ben a ghost seen in the cap'n's house;' and I heard on 't clear over to Needham and Sherburne.

"Some o' the women they drew themselves up putty stiff and proper. Your Aunt Lois was one on 'em.

"'Ghost,' says she; 'don't tell me! Perhaps it would be best ef 'twas a ghost,' says she. She didn't think there ought to be no sich doin's in nobody's house; and your grandma she shet her up, and told her she didn't oughter talk so."

"Talk how?" said I, interrupting Sam with wonder. "What did Aunt Lois mean?"

"Why, you see," said Sam mysteriously, "there allers is folks in every town that's jest like the Sadducees in old times: they won't believe in angel nor sperit, no way you can fix it; and ef things is seen and done in a house, why, they say, it's 'cause there's somebody there; there's some sort o' deviltry or trick about it.

"So the story got round that there was a woman kep' private in Cap'n Brown's house, and that he brought her from furrin parts; and it growed and growed, till there was all sorts o' ways o' tellin on 't.

"Some said they'd seen her a settin' at an open winder. Some said that moonlight nights they'd seen her a walkin' out in the back garden kind o' in and out 'mong the bean-poles and squash-vines.

"You see, it come on spring and summer; and the winders o' the Cap'n Brown house stood open, and folks was all a watchin' on 'em day and night. Aunt Sally Dickerson told the minister's wife that she'd seen in plain daylight a woman a settin' at the chamber winder atween four and five o'clock in the mornin', – jist a settin' a lookin' out and a doin' nothin', like anybody else. She was very white and pale, and had black eyes.

"Some said that it was a nun the cap'n had brought away from a Roman Catholic convent in Spain, and some said he'd got her out o' the Inquisition.

"Aunt Sally said she thought the

minister ought to call and inquire why she didn't come to meetin', and who she was, and all about her: 'cause, you see, she said it might be all right enough ef folks only know'd jest how things was; but ef they didn't, why, folks will talk."

"Well, did the minister do it?"

"What, Parson Lothrop? Wal, no, he didn't. He made a call on the cap'n in a regular way, and asked arter his health and all his family. But the cap'n he seemed jest as jolly and chipper as a spring robin, and he gin the minister some o' his old Jamaiky; and the minister he come away and said he didn't see nothin'; and no he didn't. Folks never does see nothin' when they aint' lookin' where 'tis. Fact is, Parson Lothrop wa'n't fond o' inter-ferin'; he was a master hand to slick things over. Your grandma she used to mourn about it, 'cause she said he never gin no p'int to the doctrines; but 'twas all of a piece, he kind o' took every thing the smooth way.

"But your grandma she believed in the

ghost, and so did Lady Lothrop. I was up to her house t'other day fixin' a door-knob, and says she, 'Sam, your wife told me a strange story about the Cap'n Brown house.'

"'Yes, ma'am, she did,' says I.

"'Well, what do you think of it?' says she.

"'Wal, sometimes I think, and then agin I don't know,' says I. 'There's Cinthy she's a member o' the church and a good pious gal,' says I.

"'Yes, Sam,' says Lady Lothrop, says she; 'and Sam,' says she, 'it is jest like something that happened once to my grandmother when she was livin' in the old Province House in Bostin.' Says she, 'These 'ere things is the mysteries of Providence, and it's jest as well not to have 'em too much talked about.'

"'Jest so,' says I, – 'jest so. That 'are's what every woman I've talked with says; and I guess, fust and last, I've talked with twenty, – good, safe church-members, – and they's every one o' opinion that this 'ere oughtn't to be talked about. Why, over to the deakin's t'other night we went it all over as much as two or three hours, and we concluded that the best way was to keep quite still about it; and that's jest what they say over to Need-ham and Sherburne. I've been all round a hushin' this 'ere up, and I hain't found but a few people that hedn't the particulars one way or another.' This 'ere was what I says to Lady Lothrop. The fact was, I never did see no report spread so, nor make sich sort o' sarchin's o' heart, as this 'ere. It railly did beat all; 'cause, ef 'twas a ghost, why there was the p'int proved, ye see. Cinthy's a church-member, and she see it, and got right up and sarched the room: but then agin, ef 'twas a woman, why that 'are was kind o' awful; it give cause, ye see, for thinkin' all sorts o' things. There was Cap'n Brown, to be sure, he wa'n't a church-member; but yet he was as honest and regular a man as any goin', as fur as any on us could see. To be sure, nobody know'd where he come from, but that wa'n't no reason agin' him: this 'ere might a ben a crazy sister, or some poor critter that he took out o' the best o' motives; and the Scriptur' says, 'Charity hopeth all things.' But then, ye see, folks will talk, – that 'are's the pester o' all these things, – and they did some on 'em talk consid'able strong about the cap'n; but somehow or other, there didn't nobody come to the p'int o' facin' on him down, and savin' square out, 'Cap'n Brown, have you got a woman in your house, or hain't you? or is it a ghost, or what is it?' Folks somehow never does come to that. Ye see, there was the cap'n so respectable, a settin' up every Sunday there in his pew, with his ruffles round his hands and his red broadcloth cloak and his cocked hat. Why, folks' hearts sort o' failed 'em when it come to say in' any thing right to him. They thought and kind o' whispered round that the minister or the deakins oughter do it: but Lordy massy! ministers, I s'pose, has feelin's like the rest on us; they don't want to eat all the hard cheeses that nobody else won't eat. Anyhow, there wasn't nothin' said direct to the cap'n; and jest for want o' that all the folks in

Old-town kep' a bilin' and a bilin' like a kettle o' soap, till it seemed all the time as if they'd bile over.

"Some o' the wimmen tried to get somethin' out o' Quassy. Lordy massy! you might as well 'a' tried to get it out an old tom-turkey, that'll strut and gobble and quitter, and drag his wings on the ground, and fly at you, but won't say nothin'. Quassy she screeched her queer sort o' laugh; and she told 'em that they was a makin' fools o' themselves, and that the cap'n's matters wa'n't none o' their bisness; and that was true enough. As to goin' into Quassia's room, or into any o' the store-rooms or closets she kep' the keys of, you might as well hev gone into a lion's den. She kep' all her places locked up tight; and there was no gettin' at nothin' in the Cap'n Brown house, else I believe some o' the wimmen would 'a' sent a sarch-warrant."

"Well," said I, "what came of it? Didn't anybody ever find out?"

"Wal," said Sam, "it come to an end

sort o', and didn't come to an end. It was jest this 'ere way. You see, along in October, jest in the cider-makin' time, Abel Flint he was took down with dysentery and died. You 'member the Flint house: it stood on a little rise o' ground jest lookin' over towards the Brown house. Wal, there was Aunt Sally Dickerson and the Widder Bije Smith, they set up with the corpse. He was laid out in the back chamber, you see, over the milk-room and kitchen; but there was cold victuals and sich in the front chamber, where the watchers sot. Wal, now, Aunt Sally she told me that between three and four o'clock she heard wheels a rumblin', and she went to the winder, and it was clear starlight; and she see a coach come up to the Cap'n Brown house; and she see the cap'n come out bringin' a woman all wrapped in a cloak, and old Quassy came arter with her arms full o' bundles; and he put her into the kerridge, and shet her in, and it driv off; and she see old Quassy stand lookin' over the fence arter it. She tried to wake up the widder, but 'twas towards mornin', and the widder allers was a hard sleeper; so there wa'n't no witness but her.'

"Well, then, it wasn't a ghost," said I, "after all, and it *was* a woman."

"Wal, there 'tis, you see. Folks don't know that 'are yit, 'cause there it's jest as broad as 'tis long. Now, look at it. There's Cinthy, she's a good, pious gal: she locks her chamber-doors, both on 'em, and goes to bed, and wakes up in the night, and there's a woman there. She jest shets her eyes, and the woman's gone. She gits up and looks, and both doors is locked jest as she left 'em. That 'ere woman wa'n't flesh and blood now, no way, – not such flesh and blood as we knows on; but then they say Cinthy might hev dreamed it!

"Wal, now, look at it t'other way. There's Aunt Sally Dickerson; she's a good woman and a church-member: wal, she sees a woman in a cloak with all her bundles brought out o' Cap'n Brown's house, and put into a kerridge, and driv off, atween three and four o'clock in the mornin'. Wal, that 'ere shows there must 'a' ben a real live woman kep' there privately, and so what Cinthy saw wasn't a ghost.

"Wal, now, Cinthy says Aunt Sally might 'a' dreamed it, – that she got her head so full o' stories about the Cap'n Brown house, and watched it till she got asleep, and hed this 'ere dream; and, as there didn't nobody else see it, it might 'a' ben, you know. Aunt Sally's clear she didn't dream, and then agin Cinthy's clear *she* didn't dream; but which on 'em was awake, or which on 'em was asleep, is what ain't settled in Oldtown yet."

THE END.

LaVergne, TN USA
08 September 2009

157225LV00003B/22/P